Antecedent

A novella by DL Gallie

A love story that transcends time.

Love can be instant. Intense. Everlasting.

The love between Bailey Beckett and Nate Winters is all three.

It's eternal.
It's seductive.
It's inevitable.

Each time they meet, it's instantaneous and all-consuming.

Not even William Clayton can tear them apart and over the years, he has tried—repeatedly.

Their love triumphs time and time again...until now.

Will William finally win the girl? Or will Bailey and Nate's love conquer once again?

For a love that transcends time, anything is possible.

AUTHOR NOTE

This book was originally released as part of the *Titanic Tales* charity anthology. It was only 12, 000 words and ended when – spoiler alert – the Titanic sank. This is the extended version and I have added an additional 12 000+ words and given Bailey and Nate the ending they deserve.

Please note that the beginning chapters are set in the United Kingdom and use UK English. The second half of the book is set in the United States and uses US English.

Oasis

Unequivocal Love

Five Words

Broken Rules

...and a few more as well.

THE UNEXPECTED SERIES

When it comes to love, expect the unexpected

The Unexpected Gift

The Unexpected Letter

The Unexpected Package

The Unexpected Connection

THE LIQUOR CABINET SERIES

Liquor has never been so disturbingly saucy

Malt Me (Book 1)

Tequila Healing (Book 2)

Wine Not (Book 3)

The Final Shot (Book 4)

The Liquor Cabinet: Series boxset

To love that stands the test of time, no matter the barriers.

SPECIAL DEDICATION

This book releases 18/8/18, not only is it a cool date but it's also my mum and dad's wedding anniversary. My dad loved my mum with all his heart, and she loved him just as fiercely in return. I may have only been ten when he passed away, but even at ten years of age, I saw true love at its finest. My mum and dad have an Antecedent love and one day again, they will be reunited.

Love you Mum and Dad **XoXoX**

My love for you spans over the lines of my past, present and future. You are what I love remembering, what I love experiencing, and what I love looking forward to.
~ Steve Maraboli

Antecedent

noun

noun: **antecedent**; plural noun: **antecedents**

1. a thing that existed before or logically precedes another.
"some antecedents to the African novel might exist in Africa's oral traditions"
2. a person's ancestors or family and social background.
"her early life and antecedents have been traced"

LOGIC
the statement contained in the 'if' clause of a conditional proposition.

adjective

adjective: **antecedent**

1. preceding in time or order; previous or pre-existing.
"antecedent events"

SOURCE: Oxford Dictionary
https://en.oxforddictionaries.com/definition/antecedent

NATE

"Dude, are you watching that chick flick again?" Jason says, as he shakes his head walking into the living room.

"No, I'm watching *Titanic*. The classic from 1953 with Barbara Stanwyck and Clifton Webb."

"The least you could do is watch the one with Kate what's-her-face and that dude who never wins an Oscar...at least you see tits in that one." He wriggles his bushy eyebrows at me before he jumps on the couch, placing his feet on the coffee table and settling in to watch the rest of the movie with me. Jason is as obsessed with the *Titanic* as I am. Well, I might be a little more than obsessed, but let's not worry about that.

The movie has finished, and after cleaning up the popcorn mess on the couch that Jason made, we both head to the kitchen to tidy up before bed.

"Night, Nate. I'm on the early shift tomorrow, so I'll see you in the evening."

"Cool, cool. Night, Jase," I reply with a wave. He nods and turns toward his bedroom, while I finish packing the remaining dishes into the dishwasher and switch it on.

After a quick shower, I slip on my Batman boxers and climb into bed. As soon as my head hits the pillow, I'm out cold and as usual, I dream about some dude, a smoking hot chick, and the *Titanic*.

...It's early in the morning on April tenth 1912, and the sun is just peeking over the horizon. Unlike Christmas, everyone is stirring, including the mice; not that there are any...I hope. Today, history will be made, the Titanic *will set sail on her maiden voyage, sailing across the Atlantic Ocean, from Southampton to New York. She is the largest and finest ship to ever be built, and I'm lucky enough to have a ticket on her first voyage. This journey would be complete if only I had my one true love and soul mate with me, but as usual, William-fucking-Clayton has managed to thwart my happiness...again.*

NATE

...Six months earlier

My name is Nathaniel "Nate" Winters. Life in London is tough for a guy like me, but when you have the woman of your dreams in your life, and a love like we do, nothing and no one can bring you down. I'm proud to say that I, Nate Winters, love Bailey Beckett with all my heart and for all eternity. I've been in love with her since the moment my eyes landed on her.

It was a Saturday morning in mid-November of 1911; she was strolling along the river with her father. That moment will forever be cemented in my memory: her green eyes sparkled in the morning sun, her long chestnut brown hair shining and blowing in the light autumn breeze. When our eyes finally met, time stood still. Everything around us faded away. She was it for me. I knew in that moment, with that one look, I had to have her.

It was another three weeks before I saw her again, and just like the first time my eyes landed on her, those same feelings washed over me again. This time, I manned up and made my move. Chugging back what was left of my beer, I slammed my mug on the table and walked over to her. As soon as I was standing in front of her, I became a bumbling fool. "Hhh...hi!" I stammered like an idiot.

She looked me up and down. The air around us became thick and clammy. Her gaze heated my skin, setting me ablaze with each pass. Her eyes eventually landed on mine and with a sultry smile, she sexily replied, "Hello." Never had one word held so much passion or sounded so erotic. We never got to start a proper conversation because her father came marching over. "Bailey, it's time to go," he growled, eyeing me with disdain.

Bailey, I thought to myself, what a beautiful name. Mustering up the courage, I reached out and grabbed her wrist. Ever so gently, I squeezed and with a smile, I said, "See you soon, Bailey."

Her eyes were locked with mine, her stare penetrating deep into my soul. Peeking out slowly, her tongue darted out and licked her lip, before she gently bit down. A guttural groan slipped from me; what I wouldn't do to have her tongue do that to me. With a smirk she replied,

"I look forward to it." Leaning towards me, her lips grazed my cheek for a fleeting kiss. A spark zapped between us, jolting us apart. Lifting my hand, I held the spot where her lips had just been, and I couldn't help but smile. She placed her finger to her lips, and ever so seductively, she ran the tip over her plump bottom lip, biting down on her finger. My eyes watched the movement of her finger and again I groaned. My cock twitched in agreement. This girl was fucking gorgeous and I would do anything to get to know her. Lifting my eyes to hers, I raised my eyebrows suggestively. She giggled and it was the most magical sound I had ever heard.

We stood there, in the middle of the bar, staring at one another. Our eyes were locked solely on one another; it was as if we were in a trance. The moment was broken when her father bellowed, "Now, Bailey!"

She whispered with a shy smile and wave of her fingers, "Bye." Turning her back on me, she followed her father out of McLaren's Bar. My eyes followed her as she floated across the floor in an angelic manner. When she reached the door, she glanced back over her shoulder at me and winked, just before the door slammed closed behind her. *McLaren's is now my new favourite place to drink,* I thought to myself, as I stood staring at the door with a goofy grin on my face.

A hand slaps me on the back, hard, and with a laugh Archie declares, "Dream on, dude." Pausing to take a sip of his beer, he continues, "There is no way in hell that you will land a lass like Bailey Beckett." My best mate

Archibald "Archie" Calhoun sneers, as he hands me another pint.

"I beg to differ, Arch. Bailey will be mine. I feel it in my bones," I confidently say, as a vision of her hazel eyes appears before me, and once again I'm grinning like the Cheshire cat.

"Let's agree to disagree, Nate," he replies as he chugs back the rest of his pint, slamming the empty mug down on the table. As he opens his mouth and loudly belches, with a smug smile on his face, he declares, "Your shout, Nathaniel." Rolling my eyes at the use of my full name, I turn towards the bar and order another round of drinks, my eyes drifting back to the door, in hope that my angel will reappear.

Over the next few weeks, Bailey and I continue to bump into one another, and what started out as playful, fun flirting turns into something passionate, emotional, raw, and extremely sensual. Bailey is a little minx and I am addicted. Her father has made it known, many times, that I am not good enough for his daughter. He clearly does not know his daughter like I do; the more he forbids us to see one another, the more she will go out of her way to see me. My Bailey is strong-willed, and knowing his disdain for me, she goes out of her way to throw our growing relationship in his face. The more time I spend with her, the more I fall for her, and her father will just have to deal with it. After all, the heart wants what the heart wants and mine wholeheartedly wants Bailey.

3

NATE

I'm still amazed that Bailey and I got our shot; fate somehow intervened and Bailey agreed to give me, Nate Winters, a chance. I will do everything in my power not to screw this up. We fall hard and we fall fast for one another. Never have I clicked with anyone like I do with Bailey; she's the salt to my pepper, and I have never been happier than when I am with Bailey.

We are walking hand in hand along the river, each of us subtly, or not so subtly sneaking glances at one another. What started as something fun has turned into something deep, something raw...something worth fighting for! I'm lost in thoughts of Bailey when suddenly she pulls me and drags us off the path. With her hands pressed firmly on my chest, she shoves me up against a tree, and within seconds, her lips are attached to mine. Without hesitation, I plunge my tongue into her mouth. Our tongues fight each other for dominance, but at the same time, dance in sync together. This spurs her on and she bites my lip gently before snaking her tongue back inside. Our tongues continue to caress one another as our hands wander and explore each other's bodies.

Kissing Bailey's lips is one of my favourite pastimes, amongst kissing other parts of her. Her hands slide down my chest, heading towards my hardening cock, but I take her by surprise and spin us around. My body is now cocooning her against the tree, our lips never breaking the connection. Skimming my hands up her sides, I brush past her luscious tits, over her shoulders. Cupping the back of her neck, I hold her tightly to me. Sliding my fingers into her hair, I grip tight and push her away from me. I gaze lovingly into her eyes. "You, my dear, are an evil little minx."

With a smirk she replies, "And?"

"And I love this side of you." Leaning to her ear, I nibble her lobe before whispering, "If we weren't in public, I'd lift up your skirt, free my cock, and fuck you hard and fast against this tree."

Bailey breathes deeply, her eyes darken with lust. She licks her plump ruby red lips, and whispers back, "And I'd let you fuck me hard and fast against this tree. Nate, you can fuck me hard and fast anytime you want."

Still staring intently at one another, she reaches forward and begins to stroke my cock through my trousers. Both our breathing is laboured; a groan forms in the back of my throat and escapes when I feel her hand dip below the waist of my pants. Her delicate fingers grip my dick, and she continues to flick her wrist up and down. The confined space of my pants heightens the intensity, and before I know it, I'm blowing my load in my pants with a grunt. She removes her hand from my pants and seductively she licks my cum off her fingers, that motion in itself has me hardening again.

"Mmmmmm," she moans before stepping around me, back onto the path. Resting my forehead on the trunk, I shake my head and smile. *This woman will be the death of me*, I think to myself when I hear her innocently say, "Are you coming?" Looking over my shoulder, I see her smiling with a playful expression on her face. Just as I'm about to step towards her, her face drops and then I hear her father.

"Bailey, what are you doing here?"

From my spot by the tree, I duck down and watch her. Without missing a beat, she skips over to her father. "Hi, Daddy, I'm just taking an afternoon stroll along the river. It's such a nice day." Looping her arm in his, she spins him around. "Walk with me, Daddy," she says, as she leads him away from where I'm still hidden in the bushes.

With their backs turned, I sneak out and walk away in the opposite direction. Looking back over my shoulder, I see my beloved seductively lick her finger before blowing me a kiss. Turning back around, I slam straight into William-fucking-Clayton, his glaring eyes burning into me. "Clayton," I growl.

"You're a disgrace. Making Bailey do that to you in public, you should be ashamed."

"At least I'm not a pervert watching people," I spit back at him.

He fumes at my reply, "Stay away from Bailey, Nate. You are beneath her."

"You don't know her, or me, for that matter," I retort.

"Yes, well, I don't associate with scum like you, never have and never will." Taking a step towards me, he gets up into my space. I can feel his breath on my face. "Stay away from her, Nate," he snarls, as he pokes me in the chest like the pussy that he is. If he truly loved Bailey like I do, he would have decked me. Before I do anything that I will regret, thankfully, Bailey and her father interrupt us.

"William, good to see you, son," Lord Beckett says, before he glares and ignores me. Her father seems to think that the sun shines out of William Clayton's ass and that he is the man for Bailey. I, however, beg to differ. Lord Beckett and I have never seen eye to eye. That may have something to do with the first time I met him; he found us in the garden...my head was under Bailey's dress as she was screaming out my name in ecstasy. He came running when he heard her screaming, thinking she was being attacked; in a way she was, it was just with my tongue. Not one of my finest moments, but there is no better place than between Bailey's thighs, either with my tongue or my cock. After that fateful afternoon, life here in London became unbearable. Her father went out of his way to torment me...just like William. It seems I now have two adversaries.

Life wasn't all peachy for me before that incident. Growing up not poor, but not rich, made life difficult at times. Add in the animosity between William and myself and it sure made life interesting. He and I have hated each other for as long as I can remember. It all started when he realised that my mum was a servant in his father's kitchen. After that discovery, he went out of his way to torment me, and over the years, that hatred had grown. His hatred gained momentum when he found out that I tried to seduce his sister...not that I stood a chance, because Wendy was irrevocably in love with Nancy Kane. After that day, Wendy and I struck up a beautiful friendship. She was all too happy to help me torment her brother, and I was happy to help her spend time with Nancy, away from prying eyes. When Wendy died, things with William escalated drastically.

William will take any chance he gets to throw his status in my face, but I don't give a flying fig about him and that just pisses him off even more, much to my satisfaction. My nonchalance is the greatest power I have over him, but when I see him trying to worm his way into Bailey's life, my blood boils.

My thoughts are interrupted when my angel speaks up. Just hearing her voice calms me, instantly. Looking directly at me, she sweetly and innocently says, "Nate, it's so good to see you again." She steps into my space and places a gentle kiss on my cheek, before whispering so only I can hear, "I'm wet for you right now. Tonight, our spot." Pulling back, she winks at me before turning to her father. "Let's go, Daddy, Grandmother will be expecting us home soon."

Turning back to face William and me, she sweetly says, "Nate, William," before doing a little curtsey and linking arms with her father again.

Lord Beckett says, "Gentlemen," as he and Bailey walk away from us.

My eyes follow her down the street until she is out of sight. I stand there with a huge grin on my face and a semi-hard cock. I'm snapped back to reality when William shoves me in the chest. "Do her a favour and walk away before you tarnish her name and reputation, Winters. Thankfully, my sister walked away before you could bring her down, but her dismissing you still wasn't enough..."

At the mention of Wendy, I seethe. "Fuck off, Clayton. Don't bring Wendy into this. This is between you and me, and you and me only."

Before I do anything stupid, I turn and walk away from him. He reaches out, grabs my arm, spins me around, and sucker punches me in the nose, snapping my head back. "Stay the fuck away from her, Nathaniel," he hisses at me. Stepping around me, he stalks off, leaving me standing there in shock with blood pouring out of my nose.

Watching him walk away, I realise that I would do anything and everything for Bailey. I have no doubt at all that I love her and will spend the rest of my life with her; her father and William be damned. I can honestly say that never have I felt a connection to anyone like this before. As corny as it sounds, she's it for me and I'm manly enough to admit it.

NATE

A FEW HOURS LATER, I'M WAITING FOR BAILEY AT our spot; the abandoned barn over on Hammersmith Lane. We have turned it into something special, just for us. Hay bales stacked up make a private room for us. On the ground is a blanket with pillows and a sheet for comfort, and scattered around the edge are glass Mason jars with candles; they emit light in an extremely romantic way. It's not much, but it's perfect for Bailey and me, and it's ours.

I've just lit the last candle, when my skin prickles; I feel her presence before I see her. Spinning around, my mouth drops open. When my eyes land on her, there are no words to explain how stunning she looks in this moment. The moon is beaming behind her, illuminating her beauty. I find myself grinning as she skips towards me. When she sees my face, she stops and gasps. "Oh, my God, Nate, what happened?" With a shaking hand, she reaches up and cups my cheek. Ever so gently, she rubs her finger on my bruising face and swollen nose. Leaning forward, she gently kisses my cheek and nose, leaving my skin tingling when she pulls back.

"It's nothing to worry about," I tell her.

"It's not nothing, Nate. Was it William?" she asks, as she holds my bruised cheek. I nod my head and grimace. "Why does he hate you so much?"

"Wendy," I sadly say.

"His sister, Wendy? Why?"

"He hated the friendship that Wendy and I had." Smiling, I think of Wendy and all the fun times we had together; we really had an amazing friendship. "He blames me for her death."

"But she died of septicaemia. How is that your fault?"

"Wendy and I were walking through the woods, she'd spent the afternoon with Nancy. I had never seen her so happy. She fell and grazed her leg, but she didn't tell anyone, as she didn't want to cause a fuss or get Nancy and me in trouble. Her leg got infected and she died from the infection."

"Nate, that wasn't your fault. It was an accident."

"You and I know that, but William blames me for

harbouring her secret with Nancy and encouraging it. Maybe if I hadn't, she wouldn't have been sneaking back and wouldn't have hurt herself."

"Nate, it wasn't your fault. Look at me."

Lifting my head, I look into her eyes. "You are not to blame for Wendy's death, it was a tragic accident. You doing that for her only makes me love you all the more. You always think of everyone else. William is just jealous of your good heart."

"I doubt that but thank you, Bailey. Enough about William Clayton." My eyes roam over her body, my heart rate increases, and my cheeks flush. "My God, Bailey, you look beautiful tonight," I say, as I lean forward and gently place my lips against hers for a sweet and innocent hello kiss. As usual with Bailey and me, it doesn't remain innocent for too long. My angel wraps her arms around my shoulders, pulling me closer to her. Her breasts are plastered to my chest as she deepens our kiss. Breaking our kiss, she drops to her knees and lowers my pants. Her eyes are locked on mine as she takes my semi-hard cock into her mouth. Her warm, wet lips slide over my tip, with her tongue she licks down my shaft and begins to stroke. She licks back up towards the tip. My dick is now harder than steel and I cannot wait to sink myself balls deep inside her. Her head bobs up and down my length; I run my fingers through her hair and close my eyes. When she begins to massage my balls, I moan, and without warning, I explode in her mouth. She sucks every last drop from me. Pulling back, she wipes the side of her mouth with her thumb, before she lies back on our blanket.

Lifting her hand, with her index finger she wriggles it in a come hither motion. Dropping to my knees, I crawl towards her. Pausing at her feet, I grip the bottom of her dress and slide it up her silky soft legs, placing gentle kisses along the way. Her skin breaks out in goose bumps. Her skirt bunches at her waist and I see that she is bare underneath. Her mound is glistening with her arousal. I gently skim my fingertip down her slit, and a moan slips through her lips at my touch. She thrusts her hips forward, but I pull my hand back with a smirk on my face. Staring down at her, I notice her cheeks are pink and she seductively licks her lips. "Please," she whimpers.

"Who am I to deny a horny lady?" I say, before lowering my face to her pussy. Breathing in her scent, I growl with hunger before I dart my tongue out and lick up her folds, flicking the tip over her clit. She wriggles beneath me. Gripping my head tightly, she shoves me further into her. I continue to slide my tongue up and down her, working her into a frenzy. She lets out a sexy groan when I thrust my tongue into her wet channel and insert a finger, wriggling it around and curling it up to her pleasure spot. Thrusting my tongue and finger in and out, her moans become frenzied and louder. Her pussy walls clench around my fingers and I know she's close. When I insert a second finger, and gently bite then suck her clit, she explodes, screaming my name as her climax tears through her body.

When her shudders subside, I crawl up her body and gaze down at her. Her cheeks are pink, her breath is laboured, and she has never looked more beautiful than she does at this moment in her post orgasmic glow. "You are so fucking beautiful, Bai," I say, as I lower myself on top of her and kiss her passionately. She moans into my mouth as our tongues dance together.

Pulling back, I rest my forehead against hers and smile. We lie there gazing at one another, for what feels like eternity, when all of a sudden Bailey flips me onto my back and straddles my waist. Staring intently down at me, she begins to undo the ribbon on her corset. My eyes are locked on her fingers as they slowly untie the satin holding her dress together. When I can see the tops of her breasts, I can't handle it anymore. Lifting my hands, I quickly and carefully pull the rest apart; her breasts are now free, and her nipples form stiff peaks. I take one between my thumb and forefinger and gently squeeze before I massage her breast in my hand; repeating the motion with the other breast. She begins to circle herself on my stomach before she whispers, "Make love to me, Nate."

Leaning down, she kisses me erotically. Our lips are fused together as she lifts her hips and frees my cock. Ever so slowly, she rubs herself over the tip. With one thrust of her hips, she impales herself on me, and I'm balls deep inside her. Her pussy lips hug my cock as she begins to slide up and down. Closing her eyes, she throws her head back as she continues to ride me. Reaching up, I massage her breasts again. Her hands join mine and together we massage, tug, and pull her nipples. Her thrusts become frantic as we reach our peak together, tumbling over the orgasmic cliff in unison.

We redress in silence, no words are needed; we know how the other feels, but there's one significant obstacle in the way of our happily ever after: her father.

Once dressed, we leave together. Hand in hand we walk back in the direction of the river. We are around the corner from McLaren's when we bump into the last person that we want to see: her father. "Get your filthy hands off my daughter," Lord Beckett growls.

"Daddy, please," Bailey pleads. "I love him, and he loves me. Why won't you let us be together, Daddy?"

"Bailey, you don't love him. He's manipulating you, now get over here." He is fuming with rage.

"Bailey, it's fine. Go with your father," I say, my voice stern but caring.

"No, Nate. I want to stay with you," she cries. A lone tear cascades down her cheek.

Lifting my hand, I wipe away her tear before resting my palm to her cheek. She leans into it, pressing her hand to mine and closes her eyes. "I love you, Bai," I say in a soft voice, "but you need to go with your father."

Opening her eyes, she looks up and smiles at me. Placing a gentle kiss on my cheek, she whispers, "Tomorrow, 10:00 a.m." Smiling down at her, I nod and watch her walk over to her father.

He pushes around her and gets up in my face. "Stay away from my daughter," he snarls, before grabbing Bailey by the arm and marching her down the street. I stand there and watch the love of my life walk away with her father. Before they get to the corner, she looks back towards me and sadly smiles at me. Lifting my hand, I wave at her and return her sad frown. It's in this moment that I decide, she and I need to leave...together.

NATE

THE NEXT MORNING, I GO TO HAMMERSMITH LANE to meet Bailey, but she doesn't come. The next day I head there again, and again she doesn't turn up. A sinking feeling forms in the pit of my stomach just after lunch, so I make the decision to go to her house and see her. On my way to her father's estate, I smile when I see her stepping out of her favourite restaurant, Champlain's. My smile soon falters when I see that she is with William. Our eyes meet and immediately I can tell she's sad. Her eyes don't have the sparkle they usually do, but when she registers that it's me, her face lights up. That light, however, immediately dims when William rests his hand on her lower back. The egotistical bastard walks towards me, pushing Bailey with him. He has a smug grin on his smarmy face when they stop directly in front of me. With a smirk, he snottily says, "Afternoon, Winters." In a douche move, he pulls Bailey closer to him, but I notice that she shudders at his touch.

"Clayton," I sternly reply, but I'm not looking at him, my eyes are firmly locked on Bailey. "Hi, Bai," I say with a nod.

"Hi, Nate," she says, pulling herself away from William and nearer to me. She leans into me, kisses me on the cheek, her lips lingering against my skin, and we hear William growl in disgust. She breaks the kiss and whispers, "Four o'clock." Subtly I nod just as Clayton, who I now refer to as asshat, roughly pulls her away from me. "It was nice seeing you again, Nate," she says as she sidesteps around me.

Clayton purposely shoves my shoulder as he stalks past me. It takes everything in my being to not knock him flat on his ass. Standing there, I watch the two of them walk down the street, hoping for Bai to turn back to me, but she never does. As soon as they turn the corner, my heart shatters for her. Never have I seen her so sad, so aloof. In a matter of days, William has managed to dim her spark, and in that moment, I decide that I will do anything to bring Bailey and her spark back to life...Anything!

Not taking the risk of getting caught up, I head straight to our place at Hammersmith and eagerly wait for Bailey to arrive. Unlike the previous two days, she turns up this time. As soon as she sees me, she jumps towards me and I catch her, wrapping my arms tightly around her. Even though it has only been two days, I missed having her in my arms. "I'm sooo sorry, Nate. I couldn't get away," she tearfully declares.

"Shhhh, it's okay. I know this is tough, baby, but we will figure it out. I love you too much to give up on us."

"I love you too, Nate, but I don't see how. Daddy is determined to make me Mrs. William Clayton." She sniffs and looks sadly at me. "I don't want that. I want to be Mrs. Nate Winters." When she says this, her face breaks out into a huge glowing smile and I return her grin.

Lowering my arms to around her waist, I hold her tightly to me. Pulling back, I gently place my lips on hers and I kiss her. This kiss is slow, it's sensual, it conveys all my emotions and feelings...it's us. Breaking our connection, I rest my forehead against hers. "Bai, baby, I want that more than anything in this world."

The bellowing of Lord Beckett shouting, "Bailey!" interrupts our perfect moment.

Still wrapped in each other's arms, he shouts, "Get away from that boy, Bailey!" He marches over to us, pulls Bailey from my arms, and stands in front of me, his chest heaving; rage simmering below the surface. He pokes me in the chest and growls, "I told you to say away from my daughter."

"Daddy, please," Bailey pleads, stepping in-between us. He glares down at her. "Please, Daddy. I love Nate and I want to be with him."

"Bailey, this isn't up for discussion. Head home, now. I need to have a quiet word with Mr. Winters." He pauses, but my girl is stubborn and stands her ground. "Now, Bailey!" he bellows.

"Fine," she huffs, but before she leaves, she turns to me and frantically kisses me: plunging her tongue into my mouth, wrapping her arms tightly around me. This infuriates her father and he pulls her from my embrace. "Enough. Get home now."

"I love you, Nate," she whispers, as she exits the barn, leaving me with her father.

"Sir, I..." He holds his hand up and interrupts me.

"Nate, I know you're a good kid and all, but this needs to stop. Now! Bailey WILL marry William and there is nothing that you or I can do about it." He runs his fingers through his salt-and-pepper coloured hair before looking directly at me, as he dejectedly adds, "My hands are tied, son."

My mouth drops open at this revelation. "You don't want her to marry him, do you?" I question him.

"It doesn't matter what I want. It's done. End of story," he glumly replies.

"Sir, no. I don't believe that. Bailey and I are soul mates. I feel it in my bones that we are meant to be together. Please help us?" I beg.

He says four words that leave me shocked. "Leave it with me, Nate." He turns on his heel and leaves me standing there stunned, wondering what he could possibly mean.

6

NATE

It's been ten days since Lord Beckett caught us, and I have never been more lonely and lost than I am right now. Everything changes when the Lord himself summons me to the Beckett estate for a meeting. This is either going to be great, or epically bad, but knowing my life, I'm going to bet on the latter.

Arriving at 3:00 p.m. sharp, the butler escorts me to Lord Beckett's study. When I enter the room and see whom else is there, I know that this meeting will not go the way I was hoping.

Nervously, I stand in Lord Beckett's office, waiting for someone to say something, to say anything; the atmosphere is full of animosity and angst. My heart is furiously racing as I wait to see what is going to happen. Nothing is said for what feels like an eternity, that is until Lord Beckett reaches into a drawer and shoves an envelope across the desk to me. "Take it and go, son!" he bellows.

From the corner of my eye, I see Clayton, the pompous ass, looking smug. Not moving a muscle, my jaw ticking, it's taking all my willpower to not jump over his desk and pound some sense into him.

"You heard the man, take the ticket and go, Winters. No one wants you here," he cockily adds, with a smarmy smirk on his face.

"Bailey does," I mumble under my breath.

"Look at me, Nate," Lord Beckett demands. Hesitantly, I look up and see anguish written all over his face. "I know you care for my Bailey, but if you truly love her, like you say you do, you will take this ticket and leave. Let her marry William. She'll grow to be happy with him." Swallowing hard he adds, "Surely you want her to be happy?"

"You know I do, Sir. More than anything in this world," I quickly reply.

"Then do this for us," he says, before quickly backtracking his words. "Do it for her, Nate. Do it for Bailey." That statement causes my head to snap up. Fear is etched on his face and that look cements my assumption that there is more to this than meets the eye. Add in the murderous look on William's face, and I know that I'm right on the money. But why?

Taking a deep breath, I swallow hard, and sadly I say, "Fine, for Bailey."

Reaching forward, I slide the envelope sitting on the desk towards the edge. Picking it up, I spin it in my hands as I look directly at Lord Beckett and utter, "I hope you know what you're doing, Sir." Standing up, I exit his office and turn towards the front entrance.

The office door has just closed behind me when the door across from me swings open, and I'm met with my beloved. Bailey races over to me and throws her arms around my neck, holding me tightly. "One hour, Nate, you know where," she quickly whispers, before stepping back from me, turning around, and walking towards the stairs to the second level.

Sadly smiling, I take a steadying breath, turn around, and leave. Walking down the front stairs, I head straight to Hammersmith Lane to wait for Bailey.

No sooner have I arrived, and Bailey comes rushing in behind me. Looking up, I see tears pouring down her face. "No, Nate, no," she cries, as she throws herself into my outstretched arms.

"I know, Bai. I don't want to leave either but I don't have a choice." Pulling back, I look deeply into her eyes. Instantly, they calm me. "Your father is right. He's a better match for you, Bai."

"That's bullshit, and you know it. I don't care about him, Nate. I. Love. You," she tearfully says. "I only want you," she adds, as she rests her head on my chest over my heart.

Holding her in my arms, my heart breaks. I'd give my

life for her happiness. I guess, in a way, my boarding the *Titanic* tomorrow is doing this for her. "I love you too, Bailey, more than anything in this world, but I have to go."

"I'm coming with you," she declares. Jumping up, she begins pacing back and forth. "Yes, I'm coming with you."

"You can't, Bai. For starters, you don't have a ticket." Taking a cleansing breath, I add, "Plus, William can give you a life that I can't, and I don't want to deny you anything that you deserve. You deserve the world, Bailey."

"No!" she yells. "I don't care about any of that, Nate. I want you. I love you. I don't care if we live here in our barn. As long as I'm with you, I'll be happy; together we'll be happy." My heart breaks when I see the hurt on her face at the prospect of me leaving.

Staring at her, so determined, so heartbroken, my heart beats faster and faster. For a second, I consider taking her up on her offer, but her father's words echo in my mind. With sadness in my voice, I say, "Bailey, I love you with all my heart, but I have to go. One day again our paths will cross, and when that day comes, you and I will be together forever. I feel it deep in here." Tapping my chest above my heart, I say, "You and I are fated to be together, but right at this moment in time, our journey needs to be separate."

"Ohh, Nate," she tearfully cries. Pushing me backwards, I drop onto our blanket and she sits on my lap. Wrapping her arms around my neck, she plants her lips on mine before resting her head on my chest. We stay fused together, holding onto one another as if our lives depend on it. Bailey lifts her head and again kisses me. We lose ourselves in the kiss, and I know, without a doubt, that everything will be fine.

She breaks our kiss, stands up, and straddles my lap. Pushing me back, she leans forward and kisses me again, grinding herself on me. She looks deep into my eyes and whispers, "Make love to me, Nate. Give me one final happy memory until our paths cross again. I know deep in my soul that you are it for me." She plants her lips once again on mine, nibbling my bottom lip before plunging her tongue into my mouth. Sliding my arms up her back, I run them through her hair and pull her head up. Her cheeks are flushed with arousal, her eyes ablaze with lust; I know I say this all the time, but never has she looked more beautiful than she does in this moment. She opens her mouth, but I shock her. I flip her onto her back, and a sexy squeal slips from her lips as I lower my body on top of hers. Bending down, I slam my lips against her and I kiss her passionately. We moan into each other's mouth, as our bodies wriggle and writhe together.

Breaking our kiss, I nip and suck my way across her chin, down her neck and chest. I suck her nipples through her corset, eliciting a guttural moan. She arches her back and runs her fingers through my hair, gently tugging, letting me know that she likes what I'm doing. My hands snake down her sides and I continue to kiss down her stomach. Sliding my fingers down her legs, I grip the hem of her skirt and push it up her legs, bunching it at her waist. I kiss further down her body.

Shuffling around, I shimmy myself in between her legs and look down at her. Her hair splayed in the hay, her eyes steadfastly locked on mine. "Please," she whispers.

With a smirk, I lower myself down and push her skirt the rest of the way up; my lil minx has removed her undergarments...again. Kissing her thighs, I spread her legs open and gently run my finger down her slit. Sliding it back up, I circle her clit before plunging two fingers inside her, garnering a guttural growl from her lips. She bites down on her bottom lip, closes her eyes, and a pleasured moan breaks the silence within the barn. Lowering my lips to her clit, I suck her swollen nub as my fingers continue their assault. Before long, she's tugging at my hair, screaming my name, her body trembling beneath me as her orgasm detonates. She shudders as her climax richotes from head to toe.

Her body stills and I remove my fingers. Lifting them to my lips, I lick her juices off as I stare intently at her. She raises her hand and with her finger beckons me to her. Straddling her waist, I crawl up her body, resting my arms on either side of her head, and gaze intently into her hazel eyes. Sadness washes over me when I realise that after tomorrow, I will not see her again for a long time. Lowering my lips to hers, I kiss her deeply. This kiss is slow. Sensual. Full of everything that we want to say to one another. It's perfect.

Pulling back, I whisper, "I love you, Bailey Bethany Beckett. Now and forever."

"I love you too, Nathaniel "Nate" Winters. Now and forever."

"Now and forever," I repeat with a smile on my face before I kiss her again.

Her hand slides between us and she slips her delicate fingers inside my pants and grips my cock tightly in her fist. She begins to fondle me but the confines of my clothing limit her movement. Lifting my hips, we strip off my pants, and as soon as my cock is free, Bailey begins to stroke faster. Squeezing tighter and tighter on the upward stroke. "Bai, babe, you need to stop. Otherwise this will all end before it begins."

She giggles, looks up at me, and with a smirk huskily says, "Well, what are you waiting for?" Wriggling her eyebrows seductively at me.

"Absolutely nothing," I say as I grip her wrists and pin them above her head. I line my cock up at her entrance, but I don't slip it in. Instead I begin to circle the tip around and around, teasing her. Staring down at her, I grin when she opens her mouth in protest, and then I slam balls deep into her. We both moan in pleasure. Thrusting my hips back and forth, we rock simultane-ously, like a well-oiled machine. She grips my ass, holding me tighter to her as we continue our horizontal tango. Our climax peaks at the same time and in unison we soar over the edge, screaming each other's name as the ecstasy overtakes our bodies. Collapsing on top of her, I nuzzle into her neck and breathe in her heavenly scent.

Lifting my head, I gaze into her eyes and smile. She smiles back at me before whispering, "Can you get off me, please?"

"Shit, yeah," I reply, as I climb off her and lie back

down next to her. She snuggles into my side, throwing her leg over me. Her arm drapes across my chest and she plays with the buttons on my shirt. Turning my head, I kiss her gently on her temple and whisper, "Bailey, you are..." She cuts me off, cupping my cheek with her hand, her thumb brushes along my lips.

"Nate, I know," she murmurs before she kisses me. Resting her forehead on mine, she stares down at me. "I know, Nate." She snuggles back into my side and together we drift off to sleep, wrapped in each other's arms, content and sad at the same time.

The sun shining through the barn walls wakens me, and I relax when I realise that Bailey is still with me. With a contented smile, I imagine my life like this, waking up with her in my arms every morning. Before I've even finished that thought, a wave of sadness washes over me. I realise that this will possibly be the last time ever that I see her. Not wanting to upset her, or me, I carefully slide out from beside her. Quickly I redress, and then I take a few moments to stare at my angel. With a sad sigh, I bend down and kiss her on the forehead and whisper, "I will love you now and forever, Bailey." She smiles in her sleep and seeing her so happy will forever be etched in my memory.

Standing up, I walk away from her and exit the barn, my eyes brimming with unshed tears. Stepping outside, I look up at the sun and dejectedly I shake my head, letting out a frustrated sigh. Placing one foot in front of the other, I sadly begin the walk back to my place to pack for the adventure that awaits me. With each step I take away from the barn, my heart breaks.

I'm around the corner from my place when I hear my name echoing down the street behind me. "Winters!" Spinning around, I'm met with William and his two henchmen–Storm McDermott and Brayden Bray; the three of them glare at me.

"Morning, boys," I say, taunting them with a tilt of my head. "Beautiful day, isn't it?" I'm met with silence, except for the birds nearby happily chirping. The rage coming from William is palpable. Before I have time to process anything, his fist comes flying towards my face. **CRACK** It collides with my nose, throwing my head back. The knock causes me to stumble backwards and fall to the pavement. As I blink away the black spots, I'm grabbed on either arm and held tightly. I thrash about but I'm still woozy from the cheap shot that I just received, and I don't see the second hit coming. William stands in front of me, grips my hair, pulls my head so I'm looking up at him, and snarls, "As soon as you are gone, she's mine, you fucker," and with a smirk he adds, "...till death do us part." My blood boils at that. I continue to struggle but it's fruitless, his men have me held in death grips. William punches me in the stomach before gripping my shoulders and tossing me to the ground like a piece of trash. He rears his leg back, kicks me in the side, spits on me, and walks away. Lying on the sidewalk, I watch him and his henchman walk away laughing.

I lie there, staring at the sky for a few moments before I roll to my side and push myself up. On shaky legs, I slowly make my way home. After cleaning up my bloody nose, I change my clothes and begin to pack. It doesn't take me long to pack my duffle; there's nothing really that I want to take with me. The one thing I want to take, I can't. With a sad sigh, I close the door on my room for the last time. Putting one foot in front of the other, I head in the direction of my future: my lonely future without Bailey.

As I pass McLaren's, my eyes brim with tears as it hits me that I will never see Bailey again. With my heart in tatters, I continue to the docks.

The dock is in sight when I hear my name being called. Glancing around, I can't see anyone, so I put one foot ahead of the other and I keep walking towards my future, my lonely non-Bailey future. Again I hear my name, but this time I recognise the voice. With a smile, I spin around to see a frantic Bailey racing to me. She's panting in front of me. "You can't get on that ship!" she shouts, tears cascading down her cheeks as she throws herself into my outstretched arms. "Please don't leave me. I love you, Nate. Please stay."

Dropping my duffle, I reach up with the pad of my thumb and I wipe away her tears, but my efforts are pointless as her tears continue to flow. "Shhhh, Bailey. I love you too, but I need to go, even though it pains me to leave you behind."

"You can't, Nate. Please don't leave me," she whimpers and begs me again. This right here is why I snuck away; I didn't want to see her like this. Wrapping my arms around her, I pull her close to my chest and hold her tightly for the last time.

Stepping back, I grip her cheeks with my hands. I lower my lips to hers and I kiss her with everything I have. Breaking our kiss, I rest my forehead against hers. Closing my eyes, I breathe her in, and quietly whisper, "I will always love you, Bailey, always from here to eternity and beyond, but I must go."

"If you love me, you will not get on that boat, Nate. Please?" she begs, her eyes are full of fear.

Before I can reply, a stern voice yells from behind her, "Bailey, get away from that boy, now!"

Looking up, I see her father glaring at us. She spins on her heel, places her hands on her hips, and says, "Father, I love him. I'm going to America with him."

Tugging on her arm, I spin her around and gaze into her hazel eyes. "You really want to come on the *Titanic*? Start a new life in America with me?"

Nodding her head, she replies, "Yes, with all my heart, Nate," as she wraps her arms around me tightly.

I'd love nothing more than for her to come with me, but I cannot offer her the life that he can. As much as it kills me to do so, I again push her towards her father, who is silently pleading with me to do so. "No, Bailey, you must stay here."

"For the first time ever, I agree with him. Bailey, you need to stay here and marry William." Lord Beckett's face is pained as he says this, before sternly adding, "That is final."

"No, Father, please?" she begs. My heart breaks

seeing her like this, but I know I must do this for her. "Please, Daddy, please," she begs again as I push her into her father's arms. When she is in his grasp, he grabs her wrist and pulls her away from me.

Bending down, I pick up my duffel and I walk away from my one true love.

With each step I take, my heart breaks.

With each cry I hear from Bailey, my heart shatters.

With each breath I take, a piece of me dies.

It takes all the willpower I have to keep going, but I know that I must do this, even if it pains me to do so. Finally, I'm in line to board and I can no longer hear her cries. Instead, I hear excited murmurs of the passengers, the staff is issuing commands, goodbyes are uttered, tears are shed—both happy and sad, while those on shore cheer in excitement and glee. It's exhilarating, but at the same time saddening.

Walking away from Bailey is the hardest thing I have ever done in my life but I know that I am doing the right thing...I hope.

Once checked in, I make my way to the upper deck. Walking over to the starboard side, my eyes take in the scene before me, and I'm still amazed that I'm doing this. I'm currently standing on the top deck of the grandest ship in the world, about to start my next adventure, but rather than happiness and excitement coursing through my veins, I have heartbreak and despair.

The engines roar to life, and soon enough, we pull away from the dock and we are on our way, finally the *Titanic* sets sail for New York. The fanfare from those on land as we depart is grand, just like the ship, and for the first time since boarding, a small smile escapes my lips. Staring out at to sea, I watch as we sail away from Southampton. My heart shatters once again and I sigh as a lone teardrop lands on the handrail.

7

BAILEY

WAKING UP WITH A SMILE, I STRETCH OUT AND MY body aches from head to toe—not in a 'Oh my God I'm dying' way, but in an 'Oh My God, I had the best night of my life. I want to do it again' kind of way. Closing my eyes again, I reach over to where Nate is, but I'm met with nothing but a cold sheet. My eyes pop open. I look around our barn and my heart shatters. Nate is gone. "No!" I shout to the empty space.

Readjusting my clothing, I race out into the morning light and sprint back into town to find and stop Nate. I've never run as fast as I am right now. Heading straight to

Nate's, I bang on his door. "Nate, open up, it's me!" I shout. I continue to pound on his door, but I know in my heart he's not here. Resting my head on the cold timber, a tear falls down my cheek, splashing on the pavement below when I hear a ship's horn bellowing in the distance.

Turning on my heel, I race down the street towards the Southampton docks. Rounding the corner at the end of the street, I see the back of Nate's head and I yell out, "Nate! Nate!" I shout it over and over. It seems everyone but him turns around. With one final shout, "Naaaaaaate," he looks over his shoulder. Our eyes lock, and just like the first time we met in McLaren's, everything else fades away and it's just us. He is frozen staring at me as I race to him, tears pouring down my face. When I'm in jumping distance, I leap and throw myself at him. He quickly drops his duffle and catches me, wrapping his arms tightly around my waist.

Lowering my legs, I pull back and stare at him, tears streaming down my face. He lifts his hand and with his thumb, he wipes away my tears. We stare at one another before he envelops me in his arms and I melt into him. Nate whispers sweet nothings to me and I beg him to stay, but he is just as stubborn as I am and says he has to go 'for me blah blah blah.' I don't understand why he keeps saying that. He and I are meant to be together: I feel it with every fiber of my body, with every kiss, with every touch; we are two halves of a whole. The kiss he just gave me proves that. His hands are still gripping my cheeks when he whispers, "I will always love you, Bailey, but I must go."

"If you love me, you will not get on that boat, Nate. Please?" I plead, but Daddy bellowing at us interrupts the moment.

Turning around, once again I beg for him to let me be with Nate, but my pleas fall on deaf ears. I must be in some parallel universe because Nate is now agreeing with Daddy. "Please, Nate. Let me come with you?" I beg once again. He grips my cheeks, tenderly places his lips on mine, and kisses me possessively one last time before he pushes me towards my father. Daddy holds me to his chest as Nate bends down, picks up his duffle, and walks away from me...from us.

My one true love just shattered my heart into a million tiny pieces.

Daddy wraps his arms tighter around me and whispers, "Shhhh, Princess, it will be all right. Trust me."

All of a sudden, I notice William next to Daddy and this causes me to cry harder. My father grips me tighter, almost painfully. Vaguely I hear him telling William to go and that he will look after me. "Thanks, Daddy," I whisper, as he and I walk away from William.

After a few blocks, Daddy stops suddenly and I realise that he and I have looped back around to the dock. He digs into his jacket pocket and places an envelope in my hands. "Go, Princess," he says, sadly staring at me. He wipes at my wet cheeks. "Go be with him."

"But, Daddy. What? Why? How?" I'm so confused right now.

"I don't have time to explain fully, but you having to marry William is all my fault. I got into trouble and his family bailed us out, on the proviso that you marry him. I never wanted this for you, Bailey. Since your mother passed, I've been so lost and made some bad decisions, but that doesn't matter right now, Princess. Go and be with Nate."

My eyes lock on Daddy and I see regret in his stare. "But how, Daddy?"

"When William decided that we needed to get rid of Nate at any cost, I knew I couldn't let you marry him, no matter the consequence. I came up with the idea of sending him away. I just failed to mention that it would also be with you. When I got the tickets, I got two. I was always sending you with him, but I couldn't tell you, or him. I needed William to believe and trust that I was heeding his orders, doing as I was told. Following his demands." Daddy grips my cheeks, kisses the tip of my nose, and whispers, "I'm sorry, sweetheart, so very sorry."

"What about you, Daddy? Come with us."

He pulls me in for a hug. "Sweetheart, I would if I could, but I need to stay here. I'm aware of the consequences, but your happiness is all I care about."

The ship's blaring horn snaps me back to reality. "Ohh, Daddy, I love you so much. Once we are settled, I'll send word to you."

"No, Bailey, don't worry about me. You go and live the life you were always meant to have with Nate. I will be fine. But you must go...now. Just remember that I will always love you, Princess, always and forever."

"I love you too, Daddy, always and forever," I say. Hugging him one last time, I take the bag he hands me, turn towards the docks, and run. I race towards the grandest ship to ever be built and my happily ever after. As I'm in line to board, a gunshot rings out from the direction I had just come from, and I know that Daddy is gone.

My eyes well with tears as I step onto the ship.

My heart breaks, but at the same time, it also beats faster.

I'm sad for Daddy and everything he sacrificed for me, but I'm excited for the adventure ahead of me.

After placing my bag on the bed, I look around our suite and notice that Nate hasn't been here yet. If I know him, I know exactly where he will be. Exiting our room, I walk down the corridor and I'm met with the most exquisite staircase I have ever seen. The two-storey high staircase has a magnificent wrought iron and glass dome overhead, complete with a chandelier. The sunlight casts a natural brightness on the staircase during the day, while I'm guessing the chandelier will illuminate the dome from behind in the night; it's truly spectacular. The staircase and bannister are built from English oak and are adorned with iron embellishments that are very Louis XIV styled. To some it's over the top, but to me, it fits the ship perfectly.

Placing my hand on the bannister, I run it along the smooth timber as I climb the staircase and make my way to the upper levels...and Nate. Pushing open the doors, I step out onto the upper deck. Over by the railing, I see

Nate staring out at sea, exactly where I knew he would be.

Just like the first time I saw him, my heart skips a beat. He is leaning on the railing, his trousers taut across his buttocks, his hair flapping in the wind as the *Titanic* sets sail for the first time. He takes my breath away. With a smile, I put one foot in front of the other and begin walking over to him. I become nervous and everything around me is heightened. The erratic beating of my heart, the roar of the engines, the excited murmurs of fellow passengers, and the screaming of those on the dock is deafening. I can hardly hear a thing. Twelve paces later, I'm standing behind Nate. Hesitantly, I lift my hand and place it gently on his lower back. He flinches beneath my touch. He spins around and when our eyes lock, I know without a doubt that I'm exactly where I am meant to be. I made the right choice.

Nate's face breaks out into the biggest smile, and like I always do, I throw myself into his arms. Neither of us utters a word. We just hold onto one another, completely content and happy to be reunited.

Eventually, we pull apart and Nate grips my cheeks and gently places his lips against mine. He kisses me like this is our first kiss. I lace my arms over his shoulders and pull him in closer. This kiss is full of passion. This kiss is Nate and me. This kiss is perfect.

He breaks our kiss. "How are you here, Bai?"

My eyes well with tears at his question, and I wrap my arms around him and begin to cry. Sadly, I think of Daddy and I know that he's gone. The tears continue to flow down my cheeks as Nate takes my hand and leads us over to the lounges lining the upper deck.

Nate lies back and I settle between his legs. He wraps his arms around me and gently kisses my ear. Taking a calming breath, I tell him everything that happened after he walked away from Daddy and me.

8

NATE

Bailey is here.

My Bailey is standing in front of me, on the *Titanic*...with me. I can hardly believe it. It feels like a dream but she is really here. My arms are wrapped tightly around her, and I listen intently as she tells me everything.

Bailey and I watch the mainland disappear, and when the air chills, we head inside and take my duffel to our cabin. After we cement our reunion as a couple, we head out and explore the ship. We are in awe. Never have we seen anything so magnificent in all our lives. We act like honeymooners; we are so very much in love. I'm extremely happy and it's all to do with the magnificent woman next to me. She charms anyone and everyone that we come into contact with; I like to call it *the Bailey effect*. I was under her spell from the moment I laid my eyes on her by the river that afternoon, and I will be until my last breath; she's it for me.

Like we do most evenings, after dinner, Bailey and I head to the upper deck, lie on the top deck lounges, and stare up at the night sky. Never have I seen so many stars. On the fourth night, we are gazing up at the sky when there is an almighty crash and the ship shudders violently. All of a sudden, a huge iceberg passes extremely close to the ship. Ice chunks break off, littering the deck. "What on Earth?" Bailey and I say in unison. Hopping up, we race to the edge to have a look. When I see how close the iceberg is to the ship, a plunging feeling develops inside of me, and I know that we are in trouble.

My sinking feeling has literally come true; the *Titanic* is sinking. The ship collided with the iceberg that Bailey and I saw, and come morning, the grandest ship in the world will no longer be floating. She will lie at the bottom of the Atlantic in her final resting place.

The following few hours are crazy and chaotic. People are frightened. The staff is trying their hardest to calm everyone and keep everything in order, but as time goes by, it's becoming more and more hectic as people become desperate to survive.

After helping a few people, we head back to our cabin. Once inside, we sit on the bed. Bailey is shaking from fear. "Nate, what are we going to do?"

Shaking my head, I quietly reply, "I'm not sure, Bai. But whatever we decide, we will do it together." We sit in silence for a few moments, and then I say, "We need to get to the boats and get to safety. I have a really bad feeling, Bai, and if we sit here moping, it won't do us any good."

After making our decision, we grab our life vests and head up to the lifeboats. On our way up, we pass Mr. Andrews in the corridor; he looks broken, defeated almost. Bailey and I had gotten to know him quite well over the last four days. He sees us and when he realises that it's Bailey and me, he races over to us. "Bailey, my dear, you need to get off this ship. The *Titanic* will sink," he sadly says.

"But...but they said it's unsinkable," I state.

"I thought so too but I was wrong, so very wrong," he quietly says. "Bailey, I'm sorry that I didn't build you an unsinkable ship." He hugs Bailey, shakes my hand, and walks away from us towards the first class smoking room. That was the last we, or anyone, ever saw of him.

Tugging on Bailey's arm, I hurriedly say, "We have to go, Bai."

Bailey sadly glances to Mr. Andrews before looking at me and nods. "Let's go," she says, squeezing my hand, and we head towards the doors leading to the deck outside.

Bailey and I step out onto the upper deck and the scene before us is chaotic: women are screaming, children are crying, the staff is bellowing orders to get the women and children into the lifeboats and off to safety. We make our way over to one, but when Bailey realises that I cannot go with her, she refuses to get in. She storms away, leaving me standing there alone. Catching up to her, I pull her aside, grip her cheeks, and I kiss her passionately. I kiss her like this is our last kiss. Pulling back, I look lovingly into her eyes. "Please, Bailey, get into one of the rafts," I plead.

"Not without you, Nate." She grips my hands that are cupping her cheeks. "You and me, now and forever," she quietly adds.

I smile at this, placing a gentle kiss on the tip of her button nose. I say back to her, "You and me, now and forever," before I pull her in for a hug.

We are shoved aside by someone making their way to the boats. In the few moments we are lost in one another, complete and utter chaos has erupted. I decide in that moment that we need to get off this ship...and now. Looking around, the doors inside catch my eye and I have an idea. Grabbing Bailey's hand, I walk us over to the edge and look to the cold dark water below. I look up and down the corridor and realise that in a few minutes this ship will be sitting at the bottom of the Atlantic Ocean, and I refuse to go down with her; sorry captain. "Bailey, we need to jump and get as far away from this ship as possible, otherwise the current will pull us under with it. I have an idea." Letting go of her hand, I walk over to the doors leading to the bar and I rip one off its hinges.

"You can't do that! That's property of White Star Lines!" a steward shouts at me.

"Was," I smartassly reply before I throw the door

overboard. Turning back, I take Bailey's hand in mine and we stare over the railing, down to the black ominous ocean below. "On the count of three, you and I are going to jump overboard, swim to the door, and climb on. We will then row ourselves to safety and wait for the rescue boats to pick us up."

"I...I can't Nate," she stammers.

"Yes, you can, Bailey. This is just another one of our adventures," I reassure her, squeezing her hand in encouragement. She looks up at me; her eyes are filled with fear but she smiles. She turns towards me, grips my cheeks, and kisses me. "I love you, Nate. Let's do this before fear takes over."

"That's my girl," I proudly say, before I take a deep breath and lift her over the railing. Once she steadies herself, I climb over next to her. Looking towards her, gripping her hand tightly, I say, "On three." I don't give her a chance to reply before I begin the countdown. "One. Two. Three." We both leap on three and we free fall into the ocean below.

With a splash, we land in the ocean. The water is colder than I expected. It pierces my skin like a thousand pins all at one time. Once in the water, Bailey and I are separated but as soon as I resurface, I call out for her. "Bailey! Bailey!" I shout over and over.

Eventually, I hear her yell, "Over here!" Looking around, I finally see her, hanging onto the door I threw overboard. Quickly I swim over to her. Gripping her cheeks I kiss her desperately, both of us chattering from the chilly water. "Nate, it's soooo cold," she stutters.

"Get up on the door, that will help." Together we both manage to climb onto the door. We lie close to one another, her back to my front. Wrapping my arms around her, we huddle together and float away from the ship that was taking us to a new life.

Soon after Bailey and I jumped overboard, the *Titanic* broke apart and she sank to the bottom of the Atlantic Ocean, taking all those still on board with her.

The air is now eerily quiet.

The water is dead calm.

It's getting colder and colder.

Bailey and I huddle together and cling to one another for warmth and security. We are frozen to our core, and even though we both know that we are highly unlikely to make it, we are together and that's all that matters.

Wrapped in each other's arms, just before dawn, Bailey and I take our last breaths and death envelops us. We float on the door until the rescue boats from RMS *Carpathia* discover us. As stories of survival and heroism emerge, Bailey and I are dubbed the "Romeo and Juliet of the *Titanic*." Our love story is as romantic and heartbreaking as it was for the famed Shakespearean couple.

...With a jolt, I wake up; tears are flowing down my cheeks. I'm frozen to the core, just like Nate and Bailey were, but most of all, my heart breaks for the couple. It's not breaking from remembering the dream. It breaks from the memory of physically experiencing it over one hundred years go.

Holy shit, I'm Nathaniel "Nate" Winters!

NATE

FOR THE NEXT WEEK, THE DREAM/MEMORY PLAGUES me every time I close my eyes. Some nights I dream from start to finish, others it's just bits and pieces all jumbled together. Each time it's more and more vivid, and when I'm awake, all I can think about are Bailey and Nathaniel —well, Bailey and me, I guess.

It's Friday night and Jason and I are heading to a booze cruise. I don't really want to go, but with my ticket, it's open bar and the money raised goes to charity so it's a win-win of sorts. After boarding, Jason finds a table and I'm on drink duty, so I head to the bar. It's pretty busy, it takes a few moments before I get served but there's no rush so it doesn't bother me. I'm staring at the bar top in my own world when I hear an angelic voice that I vaguely recognise. "What can I get for you?" My heads snaps up and I'm met with the most amazing hazel eyes and an electric smile. A feeling of déjà vu washes over me. "Have we met before?" I ask.

"I don't think so. I'm new to town," she replies, her voice seeming all the more familiar.

Without thinking, I outstretch my hand, "Hhh...hi!" I stammer like a bumbling fool. "I'm Nate."

Her head snaps up and her eyes bulge open when she hears my name. With a smile that lights her up face, she replies, "I'm Bailey, Bailey Beckett."

She reaches across the bar and places her hand in mine. I'm overcome with feelings and emotions that I have never felt before, not while awake anyway. My heart rate accelerates. My breathing becomes labored, and as I stare into her eyes, I know.

She recognizes me.

I recognize her.

We both recognize one another.

Our eyes bore intensely into each other's soul and an electric current passes between us. Memories of us from my dream vividly flash before my eyes, and I know precisely what she's feeling, she's remembering exactly who I am.

We both gasp.

She's my Bailey.

I'm her Nate.

Like our first meeting, over one hundred years ago,

everything around us disappears; it's just us. My heart swells as snippets of our love begin to pump rapidly through my mind, and I'm accosted with memories of our previous meeting, not just on the *Titanic,* like I've been dreaming, but also many different times over the years.

BAILEY

How is this possible?

How am I standing before the man I have been dreaming about?

How, after only touching this man, do I know it's him?

How, after one brief touch, do I wholeheartedly know we are soul mates and meant to be?

"I'm dreaming. This isn't possible," I mumble to myself, as I continue to stare at Nate, my Nate.

My boss shouting snaps me back into the present. "Bailey, get back to work."

Looking toward the walk-in cooler, I smile. "Sorry,

Billy." He's glaring daggers over my shoulder at Nate. When his eyes snap to me, they soften a little but he's still not happy. Looking back to Nate, I notice he's still in shock. Hell, I'm in shock. If I weren't working right now, I'd pour myself a shot of bourbon, down it, and then pour another. I can feel Billy still gazing, so I snap back to reality and get back to work. "Nate, what can I get you?"

He's staring at me intently, but it's not awkward, it feels like he's done this a thousand times before. His face is etched with confusion, shock, awe, and love. His stare penetrates my soul; I can feel it coursing through my body. It leaves me feeling warm and fuzzy.

He blinks a few times and then all of a sudden, together we say, "Beer." Both of us laugh.

"Ummm, yeah, two beers, please," he stammers, but then his face breaks out into the biggest smile. "How did you know?"

"Nate, I seem to know a hell of a lot about you. I'm betting that *Titanic* is your favorite movie and you love Hendrix."

"This is too weird, but I know you love shooting bourbon and there's a pink gloss in your pocket."

My hand pats my pocket and I grin sheepishly back at him. He is even more gorgeous in the flesh, my dreams, well memories, didn't do him justice. I look to the side and I see that Billy is still glaring at us. "Two beers coming right up."

Turning to the fridges, I lean down and grab two bottles, pop the caps, and pass them to Nate. Our fingers brush when I hand the bottles to him, and I feel a spark.

My body comes to life at his touch and I'm taken back in time as memories flood my brain...

...We had just arrived at Woodstock and the air was electric. Everyone was dancing to the music and having a blast. The five of us were walking in, when a guy leaning against a fence caught my eye, I froze midstep. He literally took my breath away, our eyes locked, and everything around me faded away. William bumped into me, and when he looked to where I was staring, he growled before linking his arm with mine and pulling me toward Wendy, Nancy, and Storm.

Looking back over my shoulder, the guy was gone. Instantly, I deflated. I was sad he was no longer there, but I couldn't shake the feeling that I had seen him before; he seemed so familiar to me. Like we had met previously.

BAILEY

...*Earlier that day*

It's the sixteenth of August 1969, and I'm getting ready to attend Woodstock with my roommates, Wendy and Nancy, her brother, William, and his best friend, Storm. The five of us get along like a house on fire, and I may or may not have a slight crush on William. I've considered acting on my crush, but he is an arrogant ass at times, and I don't need that in my life.

Pulling on my bell-bottom indigo blue jeans, red and pink bold stripe rolled up T-shirt, and my woven wedge sandals; I'm almost ready for a weekend of music and fun. Walking over to my dresser, I grab a hairband and I tie my hair into a loose braid before slipping on my floppy hat and Jackie-O inspired sunglasses. "Looking good," I say to my reflection before I pick up my Pink Plus gloss and slather my lips. Replacing the wand, I pucker up, blow a kiss to myself in the mirror, and head out to join the others.

Walking out into the room, William looks me up and down before he whistles at me. My cheeks heat with a mixture of embarrassment and arousal. "You look gorgeous, Bailey," he says, and I notice that his eyes roam over my body.

"Thanks, Willy, you look nice too." He's wearing jeans and a tie-dyed tee, his signature look, and he works it well. As I stare at him, I think to myself, *If only you weren't such a jackass. We could be so good together.*

"Looking good, babe." Wendy singsongs as she skips by me into the kitchen. On her way past, she grabs a bottle of vodka off the hall table. Following her, I grab the tomato juice, Worcerstshire sauce, and Tabasco, and place them on the counter next to the highball glasses she has started to fill with ice and celery. We work in sync together, and before we know it, we have four awesome looking Bloody Marys. Grabbing the drinks, we walk back into the living room and hand one each to William and Nancy. We all raise our glasses and yell, "Cheers."

Nancy walks over to the record player and puts on Jimi Hendrix. Spinning around, she begins to sway to the music, her hips moving in time to the beat. Out of the corner of my eye, I notice Wendy intently watching her, she is oblivious to everything else in the room, and her sole focus is on Nancy. I find myself smiling, she notices me watching her, and she quickly gets up and heads back into the kitchen. It's frustrating, watching them tiptoe around each other, I wish one of them would just make a move. They are perfect for each other, and I cannot wait until they are officially together.

There's a knock at the door, and William jumps up. "That'll be Storm." Inwardly I sigh, I'm not a fan of him because he and William bring out the worst in each other. Separately they are great guys and fun to have around, but it seems wherever William goes, he goes. I'm not quite sure why I don't particularly like him, but he seems to be the only one who can keep William in line when he becomes irrational, which lately has been often.

"What's up, everyone?" Storm says, walking into our flat as if he owns the place. He walks over to the coffee table and whips out a bag of marijuana and begins to roll a joint. "What are you doing?" I ask, my voice a littler higher in pitch than I anticipated.

"What does it look like I'm doing?" he matter-of-factly replies.

"Not in my house," I snarl.

"Chill, Bai. It's just a joint," William says. Taking a seat next to Storm, he begins to roll one himself.

"Not. In. My. House." My jaw is clenched as I spit each word out, "If you want to do that, get out," pointing to the door as I say this.

"You're such an uptight bitch, you need a hit," Storm hisses.

William laughs. Wendy and Nancy come back into

the room, both of them have flushed cheeks and I smile, but when Nancy sees what's going on her face drops. "Nope, not in this house. If you two want to light up you can leave." They stare blankly at her. "Out!" she bellows. Nancy has a gentle nature, but when you do something that she's not fond of, her wild side comes out—this is one of those times.

"Lighten up, babe. Maybe all you chicks need a hit."

Wendy, not one for confrontation, walks into the center of the room and scowls at him. "William, you're my brother and I love you and all, but not here. The girls and I don't want that here. "

"You are full of shit, dear sister. You and I had a toke just the other day." She lowers her head and sighs. Nancy's head snaps toward her and her face is full of disappointment.

"What is he talking about, Wendy?"

"Nothing, he's just being a butthead brother. Right?" Wendy is glaring at him.

"Yeah, I'm just joking around. Come on, Storm, let's go outside."

With that, they both stand up and leave. Nancy walks over to the door, flicks the lock, and when it engages, she turns around to Wendy and sadly asks, "Did you?" Wendy dejectedly nods. "You know how I feel about drugs, why, Wendy, why?"

Wendy begins to cry. "I don't know why. William was being William and I let my guard down. I'm so sorry. Please forgive me." She falls to her knees and begins to sob. Nancy races over to her and wraps her arms around Wendy.

"Shhhh. It's okay. We all make mistakes. I just don't want to lose you like I lost Stephen."

"I know, I'm so sorry, Nance. I'll never do it again. I don't want to lose you. I love you too much for that."

My eyes bug open at this declaration. Nancy's face breaks out into a super big grin. "I love you too," she whispers back, resting her forehead against Wendy's. They stare at each other for a few moments before Wendy places her lips against Nancy's, she places her hands on Wendy's cheeks and they tenderly kiss each other. It's the most beautiful thing I have ever seen. Quietly, I try to exit the room, but I trip on the shaggy rug and land next to them. They break apart and their heads snap to me.

"Hi," I timidly say. We stare at one another and then break out laughing. Once we have all calmed down, with a huge smile I say, "I'm so glad you two are together."

"You knew?" Wendy asks.

"Blind Freddy knew."

"Shit, William," she gasps.

"He's blinder than blind Freddy. He has no idea, and I think it's best to keep it that way for now. He's a total pompous ass, how you two are related is beyond me."

"I question that everyday." She pauses, takes Nancy's hand, and squeezes. "Are you sure it's okay?"

"More than okay. I've been wishing for this for months now, but it seems you two are very good at hiding things."

"Guess we will have to hide a little longer then."

"Not in this house you don't. I want you both to be happy, and I am over the moon that you've found each other. One day, I hope to find a love like you two."

"You will, Bai. And dressed like that, maybe today will be the day." She winks at me.

"Here's hoping."

Wendy, Nancy, and I step outside, where we find Storm and William leaning against his truck waiting for us. "Ready to go?" William shouts, as if the confrontation five minutes ago didn't occur.

"Yep," the three of us girls say in unison. We all break out laughing, and as we climb into the truck, I know this weekend is going to be amazing, and I hope that maybe I will meet my Romeo.

12

BAILEY

WILLIAM PARKS HIS TRUCK AND WE ALL CLIMB OUT and walk in. The atmosphere is electric. There are people dancing everywhere. People are smoking joints out in public, and I shake my head at their brazenness, but *to each to their own*, I think to myself.

Wendy, Nancy, and I link arms and we continue to walk around. William and Storm are behind us, but if I'm honest, I hope we lose them in this crowd—fingers crossed. Eventually Wendy and Nancy break away from me, and I find myself happily watching them—but not in a creepy way. Out of the corner of my eye, I notice a guy leaning against a fence, chatting and laughing with his friend. Midstep, I freeze. He is absolutely gorgeous. Dark shaggy hair. Tight jeans that accentuate his hips. His shirt is hanging in his pocket, and I'm met with a chest that was carved by the gods. I swallow deeply as I continue to stare at this fine specimen of a man. He looks up and our eyes lock on one another. The music and chatter fades away. I don't register anyone except him. He grins at me and his smile is electric. I feel it from where I'm standing, and I'm a good ten to fifteen feet away from him. The moment is broken when William crashes into my back. "Sorry, Bai," he says, but I don't react, my eyes are still locked on the guy. William looks to where I'm staring, and I swear he growls like a feral dog. Gripping my arm tightly, he pulls me away and over toward Nancy and Wendy. "Let's go, Bailey," he angrily grumbles, as he continues to pull on my arm.

Looking over my shoulder, I see the guy is gone and instantly I deflate. Pulling my arm free, I stop. "What the hell do you think you are doing?"

"You're too good for him," he spits between clenched teeth. His eyes full of rage, I can feel the anger radiating off him.

"For who? What are you talking about?"

William spins around, roughly grabs my upper arms, and snarls, "Stay away from him."

"What and who are you talking about?" I'm so confused right now, and when I look at him, I see he's staring at where the guy was. "Do you know that guy, William?"

"Just stay away from him, Bailey." Before I can press

him further, he storms away. Leaving me standing there confused.

Wendy walks over to me and slings her arm around my shoulder. "What was that all about?"

Shaking my head, I shrug. "Beats me, but your brother needs to lay off the weed. He's acting weird."

"Bai, he's always been weird." She laughs. "Now where to?"

"I need a drink and a dance."

"Sounds like a fine plan to me," Wendy says.

She grabs Nancy's hand, links arms with me, and the three of us walk toward the stage, where a band called Santana is playing. "These guys are pretty good," I whisper to them, they both nod at me and we continue to sway to the music.

After a few more songs, I lean over to Wendy. "I'm going to the bathroom and to get a drink, want anything?"

She shakes her head no and then pulls Nancy into her arms and they rock to the music together. I'm so happy they finally took a leap. I'm lined up for the bathroom and I find myself still swaying to the music. After emptying my bladder, I look for somewhere to get a drink when I shiver. I feel like someone is watching me. Spinning around, I see that right behind me is the guy from before. I thought he was good-looking from ten feet away, but up close he is absolutely stunning.

"Hhh...hi!" he stammers like a bumbling fool. "I'm Nate."

"Nice to meet you, Nate, I'm Bailey." My tongue darts out and I lick my bottom lip, gently biting it. I notice that Nate is watching me intently. My cheeks darken, and my heart rate increases. Never have I been affected by a guy before like I am with Nate. "Are you having a good time?"

"I am now," he confirms, raising his eyebrows at me before winking.

Ovaries—BOOM!

Swallowing deeply, I take a deep breath and ask, "Wanna go for a walk with me, Nate?" Never before have I been so confident or brazen with a member of the opposite sex, but Nate makes me feel at ease and strong.

"I'd love to, Bailey."

I smile back at him, I love the way he says my name. Linking arms with him, I say, "Lead the way," and we head in the opposite direction to the stage.

Our steps fall into sync. Vaguely, I hear the music and chatter of people around us, but right at this moment, all I can focus on is Nate. Eventually we stop, and I notice that we are at the spot where I first laid eyes on Nate, I laugh.

"What's so funny?" he asks.

"Umm, you were standing in this exact spot when I first noticed you." He nods his head at me. "I looked back and then you were gone. I thought I imagined you."

"I noticed you as soon as you walked in. Bailey, you are exquisite. There's this aura around you that draws people in. I wanted to race over to you, dip you back, and kiss your gorgeous glossy lips."

I blush at his words. No one has ever spoken to me like that before, and if I'm being honest, I love it. "I'd have liked that," I whisper, and before I know what's happening, Nate has me dipped back and his lips are pressing against mine. My mouth opens and his tongue ever so slowly slips into my mouth. I gently suck his before I slide my tongue into his mouth. We continue to caress each other's tongues, our lips fused together in the most sensual, erotic kiss ever. This is the best kiss of my life. All too soon, I'm upright again and I'm staring into Nate's eyes. My breathing is labored, and I swallow before I lift my fingers to my lips. "Wow," I mumble to myself.

"Wow indeed," he replies.

A force beyond my control takes over my body; I wrap my arms around his neck and smash my lips to his again. He slips his arms around my waist and pulls me in close. Our lips meld together, you cannot tell where I end and he starts. I moan into his mouth as the kiss deepens. Breaking our connection, I close my eyes and rest my forehead against him. "This is all familiar. It feels perfect."

"I agree," he whispers.

Our perfect moment is interrupted when I'm yanked away from Nate. "Stay away from her, Winters," William growls.

"Clayton, nice to see you," Nate calmly replies.

"You two know each other?" I ask, completely confused.

"Yep," Nate says at the same time that William snarls, "Unfortunately."

"William, don't be so rude," I snap.

"Walk away, Bailey. You don't want this scum in your life."

"William, I will hang around whomever I want. You are not the boss of me."

"Don't press me on this, Bailey. I—"

"Bailey, it's fine. I'll catch up with you later," Nate says.

"Like hell you will," William snarls.

Nate reaches for my hand and squeezes it reassuringly. His eyes never leave mine. He whispers, "Trust me," before leaning forward and gently placing a kiss on my cheek.

From my side, William yells, "Stay away from her, Winters!"

Turning to William, I angrily stare at him. "William, what's gotten into you? This isn't you."

Nate rolls his eyes and scoffs at this. My head snaps to his and I lift my eyebrows at him. He raises his hands in surrender, "Bai, I'm going to leave you with him." He emphasizes the word him. "I'll catch you later."

I like the way he says Bai, but I'm uncomfortable with what's going on between William and Nate, especially when William mumbles, "Don't count on it." I glare at William before I look back to Nate.

"I'd like that, Nate and I'm sorry." Nodding my head in the direction of William.

"Don't be, it's not you. It's him." He places emphasis on the word him but his eyes never leave mine.

"What is with you two?" I ask, looking between the two of them.

Neither one of them answer me. They just glare at one another. Like children. I shake my head. "I don't have time for this crap." I start walking away. Someone reaches for my hand, and without turning around, I know it's Nate. He tugs me back to him. He leans into my ear and whispers, "I'll be thinking about you until I see you again later."

I shiver at his words, but before I can reply, he's gone. I'm left standing in the middle of at least twenty thousand people and I feel lonely. I'm snapped back to reality when William grabs my elbow. "Bailey, you will stay away from him."

"Tell me why and maybe I will."

"Because," he sternly states, crossing his arms defiantly over his chest.

"Because? That's all I get?"

"Just stay away from him." Before I have a chance to reply, he storms off and, once again, I'm left standing by myself.

I'm angry.

I'm confused.

And I'm pissed off.

All my happiness from five minutes ago has disappeared, but I know one thing for certain, I want to see Nate again.

13

BAILEY

After purchasing a homemade lemonade from the drink stand, I take a sip and moan. It's the perfect combination of sweet and sour. Looking around, I see many revellers dancing and having the time of their lives. Woodstock's popularity blew everyone away and there was a chance it was going to get cancelled, but thanks to Max Yasgur—thanks, Max—he offered his land and here we are. Standing amongst the crowd, I find myself happy, but I'm not enjoying myself as much as the other partiers. I'm so confused right now. The incident between Nate and William keeps playing in my mind. And then there's

Nate, I can't stop thinking about him. I really hope we do meet up again.

Turning back around, I start walking toward the stage when someone laces their fingers with my left hand. Electricity tingles up my arm, my body heats with desire. Our hands fit together perfectly and I smile. Looking to the left, I'm met with the smiling face of Nate.

"Nate."

"Bailey."

No other words are said.

No other words are needed.

Everything in this moment is perfect.

Our steps fall into sync as we walk over to a recently vacated table and chairs and sit down. Our hands are still clasped together over the top of the sticky table, and we stare deeply into each other's eyes. Down into each other's souls. I feel like I have stared at these eyes many times before. "I feel like I know you," I whisper.

"I know what you mean. When you walked in, my sixth sense sparked to life, and then I looked over and saw you. Time stood still in that moment, and then I saw you with him and my heart deflated." His shoulders drop as he says that.

"William? He's my roommate's brother."

"So you're not together?"

I shake my head. "No, I thought maybe something would eventuate between us, but I was always hesitant 'cause he can be an ass at times." Nate laughs at this. "I'm really not so sure anymore because..." I'm looking directly at him as I say this and leave it hanging. My words register in his brain and his face lights up. Gently rubbing my thumb over the back of his hand, we continue to stare at one another. As I gaze into his eyes, I feel at ease. Even though I have just met him, it feels like I have known him much longer.

"Because you feel it too, don't you? This pull. This connection. It's like we are the missing half of the other."

Nodding my head in agreement, I whisper, "Yes."

He leans across the table toward me. I lean forward to him. Our lips meet. My tongue seeks access to his mouth and he lets me in. Our tongues dance erotically together. All the air in my lungs gets sucked into this kiss; this wonderful, amazing, make you weak at the knees kiss. It's soft. It's slow. It's sensual. It's so different to the one earlier, that kiss was rough and hungry.

Breaking the kiss, I lean back into my seat and stare across the table at him. My lips curl up in a smile, my eyes bright and my heart racing faster than ever before. *What is this man doing to me?* I think to myself, as I grab my drink and take a sip.

"So, tell me about yourself, Nathaniel."

"How did you know my full name was Nathaniel?"

Hesitantly I stare at him. "I, umm, ahh, I didn't know. I just presumed and it was obviously a lucky guess."

"Yeah, let's go with that," he replies with a wink. I feel that wink deep in my soul and a feeling of déjà vu washes over me; I swear I've seen that wink before. "Anyway, I'm your average guy. I work in construction; I'm currently working in Lower Manhattan on a building called the World Trade Center. I started just after they broke ground back in '66, and I've been there ever since. It's hard going but I love it." He takes a sip of my lemonade, and I intensely watch as his tongue darts out and swipes his bottom lip. Who knew licking a lip could be so erotic? "And what do you do?"

"I work in our family bar, Beckett's. It's been in our family for two generations now. When Daddy passes it will be handed down to me, since I'm an only child."

"I don't think I have ever drank there."

I clutch my chest and feign shock. "Well, we cannot have that. You will have to come by this week. Grandmother makes the best shepherd's pie around."

"Well then, I must stop by this week sometime." He winks at me, and again I feel it radiate throughout my body. Lifting my lemonade to my lips, I drink and stare at the man across from me. Even though I have only just met him, I feel like I have known him since the beginning of time. Never have I had a connection to someone like I do with Nate, and we seem to know things about each other that we shouldn't, considering we only met today.

We fall into easy conversation and before we know it, the sun is starting to set. "I guess I better go find my friends." I pause. "Do you want to come with me?"

"I'd love to, Bailey, but I need to meet up with my friend, Archie. He's probably wondering where I am. And I guess your friends are too."

"Yeah, I understand." I deflate at his reply, my shoulders sag.

"Bai, I would love to meet up with you again. Maybe

we can meet back here in a few hours? Say when Credence comes on?"

Immediately I smile. "I'd really like that, Nate." Standing up, I walk around the table and sit down on Nate's knee. I drape my arms over his shoulders, lower my lips to his, and I kiss him. Never have I been so bold before, but Nate brings out a side of me that I like. He wraps his arms around my waist and deepens our kiss.

Everything around me fades away. I just focus on Nate and this kiss. He brazenly slides his hand up under my shirt and squeezes my boob. Normally I'd smack the hand away, but not this time. I run my fingers up into his hair and I gently tug on the strands. We both lose ourselves in the kiss. I hold him tighter to me, my breasts squishing into his chest. His hand is now squashed between us, but he somehow manages to pinch my nipple, and this sends shockwaves straight between my legs. I clench my thighs together and moan into his mouth.

Pulling back, I rest my forehead against his. "Nate, we need to stop this before I straddle your legs and do something that should not be done in public."

"Reluctantly, I agree, but I would like to try that scenario out at a later date." He winks at me as I hop off his lap and we both stand up. We stare at one another as Nate reaches for my hands. He laces our fingers together and we face each other, holding hands; my cheeks are flushed, and once again my heart is racing like a race-horse. "But I will say, that was the best freakin' kiss of my life. Bailey, I—"

"Nate, there you are." The moment is interrupted when his friend walks up to us. "I just saw Clayton and he looks pissed off, I know you did something." He doesn't see me. "Dude, what—" He finally notices me, then looks back to Nate, "Yep, now I get it." He turns his attention back to me. "Pleasure to meet you, ma'am, I'm Archibald Calhoun, but my friends call me Archie."

"I'm Bailey. Call me ma'am again, Archie, and we won't be friends anymore."

He looks to Nate. "I like the sass on this one." He turns his attention back to me and with a cheeky grin adds, "When you get sick of this mug, come find me."

"I'll keep that in mind." I glance to Nate, before adding, "But I think I'm exactly where I'm meant to be."

"Your loss. Anyways, dude, what's up with Clayton?"

"Are you talking about William?" I question Archie.

"You know him?" Archie probes.

Nodding my head, I reply, "Yep, I live with his sister."

"That explains everything then."

"What do you mean?"

Before Archie can reply, Nate interrupts, "Ignore him, I do." He tries to subtly eye Archie to be quiet, but I notice. "He clearly got too much sun today. Bai, how about you go find your friends, and we can meet up later like we agreed to?"

Staring at Nate, I nod my head. I'm unsure of this change in him, but I do want to find Wendy and Nancy I need to discuss: A. Nate, and B. Find out the history between him and William. "Yeah, okay. I'll catch up with you here later when Credence is on."

Stepping toward him, I place my lips on his cheek. I linger a little longer than necessary, but I can't seem to help myself when it comes to touching Nate. When I pull back, I nod at Archie and walk away. With each step I take, I can feel Nate's eyes boring into me. I find myself smiling, I cannot believe how today has turned out.

14

BAILEY

Walking away from Nate, I'm in a daze. I'm sitting on cloud nine and I could not be happier. The air around me is electric and I'm not referring to the concert, I'm referring to the buzz I have from being with Nate. Don't get me wrong; everyone at Woodstock is having a great time too.

I'm not sure who is playing on stage at the moment, but everyone is grooving away and I eventually find Wendy, Nancy, William, and Storm. The four of them are swaying to the music, enjoying themselves. Nancy and Wendy have their arms wrapped around each other and that makes me smile. I'm so happy they decided to act on their feelings. If any two people should, and deserve to be together, it's them.

"Hey hey, party people!" I yell when I'm in earshot. My arms swinging above my head, my hips swaying to the beat of the music.

"You took your time," Wendy says, but when her eyes land on mine, she grins at me. "So, how was the drink? You are looking mighty refreshed."

William growls at Wendy's statement, this causes us to look at him inquisitively and immediately I remember his warning about Nate. It pisses me off, so I say to Wendy, "I kinda met someone." This garners another growl from William. Staring at William I add, "He and I are going to meet up again later."

"Do tell?" Nancy excitedly asks, pushing William to the side.

"Well, his name is Nate. He's ohh so dreamy. Like Jim Morrison hot."

"So he lights your fire?"

Nodding my head in agreement, I grin. "Actually, I saw him when we first arrived, but he disappeared and then POOF he appeared. I can't explain it, but I'm drawn to him like a moth to a flame." I gaze to the sky and grin. "I can't wait to see him again."

"Bailey and Nate sitting in a tree," Wendy starts to sing, and then Wendy joins in, "K. I. S. S. I. N. G, first comes love, then comes marriage, then comes—"

"You two can't sing for shit." William points to the stage. "Shut up and let the professionals do it," he snarls.

Wendy, Nancy, and I exchange a 'what the hell' look and shrug our shoulders.

"Well, I'm happy for you," Nancy says. "Everyone needs to find that special someone." She says that end part while staring lovingly at Wendy; seeing them finally happy together gives me hope that I will find happiness like that too...and I think I have.

"Yeah, we all do," I say, nudging her shoulder and happily winking at her. "Let's dance," I suggest, and the three of us let the beat of the music overtake our bodies once again.

This is the most amazing festival I have ever been to. I'm standing next to Storm when the hairs on the back of my neck stand on end, and I know he's behind me. Spinning around, I see Nate and Archie walking toward me. A force beyond my control engulfs me and I run to him. When I'm close, I launch myself in the air. He opens his arms and catches me. I wrap my legs around his waist and I throw my arms over his shoulders. I slam my lips into his and press myself into him. He pauses for a moment, and then he's kissing me back.

From behind me, I can hear Wendy, Nancy, and Storm hollering and a growl, which I'm going to guess is William, but I'm not giving in to him. He can suck it up and deal with it. Lowering myself down with a smile, I murmur, "Hi."

"Hi, feel free to greet me that way anytime."

"Duly noted. Come meet my friends."

"I'd love to."

We lace our fingers together and make our way over

to them. "Guys, this is Nate. Nate, this is Wendy, Nancy, Storm, and William."

William grunts and stomps away.

Storm outstretches his hand to Nate. "Nice to see you again, Winters."

"You too, Storm. You still working for what's-his-face?"

"If you mean, Jenson, then nah. I've gone into the family business."

"You, Storm Johnson, are a banker? Like in an office? Suit everyday banker?"

"Yep. The old man persuaded me to follow in his footsteps."

"And?"

"It's fucking awesome. Who knew?" He pauses before sternly adding, "Now, you take care of Bailey here, or I will be forced to kick your ass." Nate laughs and nods his silent agreement that he will not hurt me.

From behind him, William spits, "How about we just kick his ass anyway?"

"What is your problem, Willy?" Wendy snaps at him.

"He is." He turns to me and through clenched teeth snarls, "You are too good for him, Bailey, and when he breaks your heart and stomps on it, I'll be the first to say I told you so." He turns to Nate then. Stepping into his personal space, he spits in his face, "You break her heart and I will end you."

Stepping between them, I raise my hands in warning. "That's enough, William. I think you need to leave. We are here to have fun and you are currently being a Debbie

Downer. Unless you want to have fun, with ALL of us, I suggest you leave."

"I don't have to put up with this bullshit, I'm outta here." He storms off, leaving the six of us stunned.

Archie says, "I see he's still a jerk."

"I think you mean asshole," Storm replies.

"He's your best friend," Wendy reminds.

"Clearly I need my head checked. Look, let's forget all this shit and have a blast. We are at Wood-fucking-stock. Let's party like we've never partied before."

A chorus of, "WooHoo," "Yeah," and whistles erupts, and we all turn our attention back to the stage and forget all about William and his meltdown.

Nate comes up behind me and wraps his arms around my waist. Pulling me into his chest. Leaning back, I rest my head on his shoulder, close my eyes, and I lose myself to the music and the calmness that is Nate's embrace. We gently sway together, and in this moment, I have never been more content or happy in my entire life.

Nate leans down to my ear and whispers, "Wanna go for a walk with me?"

Opening my eyes, I turn my head to look at him. I gaze into his eyes and breathlessly whisper, "Yes."

Nate spins me around and we continue to stare at one another. "I'm so glad I met you here today, Bailey. I feel like I've found the missing piece in my life. Who knew I was missing a sexy blonde-haired siren?"

"Ohh stop," I say, playfully whacking him in chest. "I'm just going to tell Nancy and Wendy that we are going for a walk." Spinning back around, I walk over to the girls. "Hey, I'm just going to go for a walk with Nate."

"A walk, is that what they are calling it these days?" Nancy jokes.

"Hardy-har-har...and yes, that's what I'm going to call it." I notice Wendy is quiet. "You okay, chickie?"

"Yeah, no, not really. I'm just angry with William. He hates everyone at the moment. I want the happy Willy from our childhood back."

"Yeah, he has changed recently. Do you know the story between him and Nate?"

"Not in full, but they've hated each other for such a long time now. I don't think they even know why they hate each other."

"Boys," I mutter.

"Hence, why I like girls," she says on a laugh.

"Yeah, you do," I tease, but I notice she's still sad. "Forget about him and have fun. Today is the start of your next adventure. Don't let your brother, or anyone for that matter, ruin it."

"You are right."

"Of course I am," I declare, but I can tell that she is still thinking about William. "Look, William is William and underneath all his jerkiness he loves you to the moon and back, just remember that."

"I'm trying, but the way he spoke to Nate and you, that was horrible. For the first time in my life, I was ashamed to call him my brother. I'm so sorry he spoke to you like that."

"Do not apologize for him, Wendy. He's big enough

and ugly enough to do that himself, once he pulls his head out of his ass. Now, I'm going to go for a walk with Nate, and you are going to turn around and have an absolute blast with your girlfriend." I smile and add, "You two have fun, now go."

"Love you, Bailey," Wendy says, as she pulls me in for a hug.

"Love you too, Wendy." Looking to Nancy, I say, "You too, babe. I'm sooo happy you two finally decided to give it a go."

Wendy pulls away and puts her hand out to Nancy; she immediately takes it, lifts it to her lips for a sweet kiss, and whispers, "Me too."

"Go have fun," Nancy says. "I'll look after her." She pulls Wendy away from me and the two of them embrace. I can see the love they have for one another pouring out.

Turning around, I walk over to Nate. "Where's Archie?"

He shrugs his shoulders and laces our fingers together. We walk off, leaving the two lovebirds happily together.

With each step that we take, my heart rate speeds up. I'm nervous and excited at the same time. I can't wait to see where the night heads.

15

BAILEY

WE WALK AROUND FOR A LITTLE WHILE BEFORE WE decide to head to Nate's car for a rest. He lays out a picnic blanket next to his car. We lie down next to one another and silently stare up at the night sky. A band I have never heard of is on stage, and the music is playing softly around us. It's very mellow, and I could quite easily fall asleep, but right now sleep is the last thing I want.

Sitting up, I cross my legs and stare down at Nate. His eyes are closed. His hands are resting beneath his head. The muscles in his arms are defined, I guess that happens when you work in construction. My eyes rake over him from head to toe and back up again. "Are you staring at me?" he huskily asks.

"Maybe," I say. Leaning down I place a gentle kiss on his lips. He pulls his arms from behind his head, cups my cheeks, and holds me to him. My eyes drift closed and once again I lose myself in Nate and our kiss. When I open my eyes again, Nate is staring up at me. Pulling back, I sit up. Nate does the same and we sit facing one another.

"What are you doing to me, Bailey Beckett? I've never felt more alive in my life, and I never want to let you go."

"I agree wholeheartedly with that statement. It's hard to explain, but I feel like we are connected and we are meant to be. Nothing and no one will get in our way. Nothing."

"Bai—" I don't let him finish, I have more to say. Grabbing his hand I place it on my chest, over my heart, and hold it tightly. My other hand, I place over his, and he lifts his hand and cups mine. "You have my heart, Nate, you and only you. No one else. You are it for me. I love you, Nathaniel "Nate" Winters. Now and forever." Leaning forward, I gently place my lips against his and close my eyes. As our lips press together, a feeling washes over me; it's like we have done and said this a thousand times before.

He pulls his hands free, grips my cheeks tightly, and deepens the kiss. This kiss is everything. This kiss is now the best of my life. Our lips fuse tightly together. Gently nipping his lip, I pull back and rest my forehead against his and we stare at one another. The silence is broken when Nate whispers, "I love you too, Bailey. It feels like I've loved you since before I saw you walk through the gates yesterday." He swallows. "I feel like I know you, but it's not from now. It's hard to explain it."

"I feel it too, Nate. It's like our souls are entwined. We were destined to meet, and now that we have, I'm not ever letting you go. You are my antecedent love and I'll never let go. Never."

Nate doesn't say anything. He leans forward and kisses me. His tongue seeks access to my mouth and I willingly let him in. Kissing Nate is one of my favorite things to do. Leaning back, I fall to the blanket below and pull Nate with me. He hovers above my body, cocooning me in. Running my fingers up his neck into his hair, I gently tug and he moans into my mouth. I smile into our kiss and pull him closer to me.

"I don't want to squash you," he says between kisses.

"I don't care." My voice is husky with lust.

Before I know it, Nate has rolled us and I'm now on top of him. His hand slides under my top, my skin tingling from his touch. His other hand grips my ass and squeezes, a moan slips from my lips, and I giggle when he tickles my ribs. Sitting up so I'm straddling him, I gaze lovingly down at him. His hands are resting on either side of my hips. A force beyond my control overtakes my body, and I pull my top over my head. I'm sitting in the middle of a field full of cars, on a blanket, in nothing but my jeans and bra, and never have I felt as sexy as I do right now.

"You are beautiful, Bai," Nate whispers, my cheeks tinge pink at his words and my heart beats faster. It's beating so fast I feel like it's going to beat right out of my chest.

Leaning down again, I place my lips over Nate's. I grab his hands and place them on my boobs. That's all the invitation he needs, he gently begins to massage them. His fingers dip inside my bra and he begins to tweak my nipples. When he squeezes, it sends tingly shockwaves between my legs. I rub myself on him and the friction causes us both to groan.

"Nate, please?" I whisper.

"Bailey, we've only just met—"

Placing my finger on his lips I shush him. "Nate, I know it's crazy, but I feel like I've known you forever. I want this. I want you." As I'm saying this, I reach behind me and unhook my bra, the straps fall down my arms and his eyes drop to my bare breasts. The cool night air hardens my nipples to form taut peaks. Nate swallows deeply before leaning forward and taking a nipple into his mouth. My eyes close. My head drops back, effectively thrusting them forward into his face. He lifts his hand and massages the one he's not currently sucking on. He alternates between them; I'm ready to explode. "I'm ready," I whisper moan as I stand up and remove my jeans and panties.

Nate leans back on his arms and stares up at me. His eyes open wide as his gaze takes in my naked form. Squatting back down, I shimmy up his legs and make quick work of his undoing his jeans. He lifts up and helps me pull them down his thighs. His cock springs free, the tip glistening in the moonlight. I swipe my finger over the tip and lift it to my lips and suck. I shuffle forward and push Nate down to the blanket. Lifting onto my knees, I hover over his cock before I slowly sink down. We both moan, he fits me perfectly. We begin to rock back and forth, our eyes locked on one another. He grips my hips tightly, while I throw my head back in ecstasy as I continue to ride him. Suddenly my skin is alight and my orgasm ricochets through my body. I moan into the night sky, and as I'm coming back to earth, I feel Nate tense beneath me. He closes his eyes and he lets go. I'm mesmerized, watching him come and the immense pleasure on his face makes me smile. His body goes limp, and when he opens his eyes, he reaches up, cups my head, and kisses me. Wrapping his arms tightly around my back, I do the same and we lose ourselves is this kiss—I never want this moment to end.

Lifting off Nate, I snuggle into his side and lay my head on his chest. This moment is perfect, and it's one that I will remember for the rest of my life. We fall asleep together and when we wake again, the sun is shining and it's all quiet on the stage. The next artist won't appear until later this afternoon, so Nate and I redress and head back in. We walk around for a bit and chat about our lives. With each word that leaves his lips, I fall more and more in love with him. He has a heart of gold, and when he looks at me, he really sees at me. It's like everything around him fades away, and I'm the only thing that he sees. I've never felt so special or wanted before in my life. And it's exactly how I feel with Nate too.

Another night passes, and I realize that I haven't seen my friends since yesterday. I have literally been wrapped up with Nate, and if I'm honest, I haven't missed them at all. "What do you say we get some food and then try and find your friends? It's been a while since we have seen them."

I look at him and laugh. "Are you in my head? I was just thinking about them."

"You're in my head, I can't stop thinking about you, Bai."

My cheeks darken at his words and I become shy. I'm not a fan of the attention but with Nate, I kinda like it. "Okay, let's get burgers and then we can go find Wendy and Nancy."

"Sounds like a plan." He laces our fingers together and we head off in search of burgers, which—by the way—are the best cheeseburgers I have ever eaten.

After eating our burgers, Nate and I head back toward the main area in search of my friends. We are so wrapped up in each other, we don't notice Wendy and Nancy walking toward us. Our moment is broken when Wendy tugs on my arm. "Bailey, babe, you need to come now. Jimi is about to take the stage and we have to see him live. He is the whole reason that you and I came." She pauses and then adds, "We.Have.To."

Stopping, I stare at her. All of a sudden I'm dog-tired, but Jimi is about to take the stage and there is no way in hell I'm missing Jimi. Wiping my eyes, I shake my head and grin at her. "I'm coming, Wendy." Looking to Nate, I ask, "You wanna come with us?"

With a smile that sets me ablaze, he says, "I'd love to." He grabs my hand; we entwine our fingers together, and follow Wendy and Nancy to the stage for the performance of a lifetime.

16

BAILEY

Jimi Hendrix was beyond awesome. He was definitely the highlight of Woodstock for me, closely followed by Credence. Daddy would have loved that, and I can't wait to have dinner with him tomorrow night and tell him all about it. Or gush about Nate.

People are starting to leave, but we don't want to get crushed in the crowd, so we hang around and wait. It's not like getting out of the parking lot will be any easier. "I'm just going to the bathroom," I tell the group and walk off.

I'm on such a high at the moment. This day, no week-end, has been beyond amazing. Not only did I get to see all my favorite bands play live, but I have met a wonderful man. A man who I can see myself spending the rest of my life with.

I'm on my way back to the group, when someone pulls on my arm and drags me between two tents. When we stop, I look up and I see William. His eyes are feral and I can feel the anger radiating off him. He's silent as he stares at me; it's extremely unnerving.

"William, what's going on?" I ask.

He still doesn't say anything; he stares right through me. It like he's here but his mind is elsewhere. His breathing is deep and ragged. His body is tense with rage and I'm really uncomfortable right now. I have never seen William like this before, and I'm beginning to get scared.

"Bailey," he snarls between clenched teeth. "You are meant to be with me." He pokes himself in his chest. "Me. Not that asshole Nathaniel-fucking-Winters."

"William, I—" He cuts me off and steps in front of me. I can feel his breath on my face and my heart rate speeds up. My body becomes clammy and sticky as the fear spreads through my veins. The air around us is thick with hate and animosity. My eyes dart around, I glance over his shoulder, trying to find a way out of here but he has me blocked in.

"Just shut it, Bailey, and you listen to me. He is not the one for you, I am." He pokes himself in the chest again.

"William, I—"

"I said shut the fuck up." He steps toward me, my panic spikes and I take a step back in fear. "You are too good for him. You and I belong together, we always have. If he hadn't swooped in, you would be mine." He roughly grabs me by my upper arms, pulls me closer to him, and slams his lips forcefully against mine. Clamping my lips shut tight, I refuse him entry. I close my eyes and try to wriggle free, but his grip on my arms is really tight. He angrily pulls back, raises his hand and slaps my face. He then sneers, "Let me in, Bailey." Then he slams his lips to mine once again, and he loosens his grip on my arms, so I push him away.

Shaking my head at him in disgust, the first tear falls down my cheek. I wipe it away and will myself not to cry. "No, William. Please don't do this." He glares at me again, and when I look up at him, I don't see the nice, friendly William that I know. Instead, I see monster William. He raises his right arm again and slaps my left cheek, my head snaps to the side, and I let out a yelp in shock.

"See what you make me do," he growls at me. "Bailey..." he says, stepping near me again. I take a step back in fear and this only aggravates him further. He grabs my arms again and pulls me to him. He tries to kiss me again but I turn my head, this only angers him more. He squeezes my arms tighter before he shoves me to the ground. I land on the grass with a thud, but before I have a chance to register anything, William pushes me down and is straddling my legs. I try and get up, but he pushes me back to the dirt. The grass is cold beneath me, and I try and focus on that, but all I can concentrate on is William and what is going to happen next.

William lowers himself over me, one hand resting beside my head, caging me in. The other hand is roughly groping my breast through my top. My eyes well with tears, everything is blurry. I close my eyes and take a deep breath when I feel him slide up my legs. His erection is pressing into my stomach when he leans down and tries to kiss me again.

Blinking away my tears, I shake my head and beg, "Please, William."

He mistakes my plea as me giving myself to him, and with a sinister smile he says, "I knew you'd come round."

Leaning down, he tries to kiss me again, when all of a sudden the pressure of him on top of me is gone, and I'm alone lying in the grass. Everything around me is muffled, but I vaguely hear someone yelling, "You asshole, get your hands off her."

Looking over, I see Nate and Archie dragging William away. Nancy and Wendy come rushing over to me. I roll onto my side, close my eyes, and I huddle into a ball. Wendy touches my shoulder and I flinch. "Bailey, it's me, you're safe now."

Opening my eyes, I look up and see both Wendy and Nancy crouched next to me, their faces full of fear. My brain kicks into gear again, and I register that it's them. Sitting up, I wrap my arms around Wendy and cry. The tears flow down my cheeks as I huddle into her. Everything around me becomes fuzzy as I let the tears and grief overtake me. Nancy slips her cardigan off and drapes it over my shoulders. I look down to see my top has been torn; my bra is not in place, and my breasts are on display.

Reaching up, I grip the edges of the sweater and hold it tight to me.

I'm tugged from Wendy's embrace as Nate pulls me into his body. His chest is erratically rising and falling, his breathing labored. "Bai, babe, are you okay?"

I nod my head that I'm fine, but to be honest, I'm not sure how I feel right now. Nate leads me over to a table, sits down, and pulls me onto his lap. He holds me tightly and his embrace is exactly what I need right now.

William walks toward us and I feel Nate tense under me, William is about to speak to us when Wendy grabs his arm and drags him away. I'm so thankful for her at the moment, I'm not ready to speak to him yet. I knew William liked me and prior to today, I kinda sorta liked him too, but then I met Nate and everything changed.

From where we are sitting, I hear Wendy letting loose on William. "You are my brother and I love you, but right at this moment, I have no words to describe how I feel about you. None. What you just did is unforgivable, and if Bailey never speaks to me again because of you, I will never forgive you. Now just go, you are not wanted here." He lowers his head and walks away, he doesn't look up at anyone. I cannot believe it, but I actually feel sorry for him. This causes me to laugh.

"What's so funny?" Nate says, his face etched with a mixture of anger and sadness.

Never in a million years will I tell him what I just felt for William. I shake my head and sadly smile at him. "It's nothing, can you please take me home?"

"Of course." He stands up and instinctively I wrap

my legs around his waist and snuggle into him. Pulling back, I stare into his eyes and I know that I will be fine. "Nate, put me down. I can walk."

"I know you can, but I like having you in my arms, Bai."

"I like it too, but please, I want to walk." He reluctantly lowers me to the ground and outstretches his hand to me. I place my palm in his and he pulls me into his side. He wraps his arm around my shoulders and hugs me for dear life. This causes the dam walls to break once again and I begin to cry. "Shhhhh," he coos. He pulls me to him and instinctively, I wrap my arms around his waist and he holds me tighter.

"I was so scared, Nate. So scared. I never thought William would do something like that. Never."

"It's over now and you are safe with me, Bai. I will never let anything like that happen to you again. I'm just glad that I was there."

"Me too, Nate, me too."

Wendy walks over to us. "Bai, I'm so sorry about my brother. He's such an asshole, I can't believe he did that. If you want me to move out, I totally understand."

"Wendy, no," I say, pulling away from Nate. "You are my best friend and I don't want this to ruin that. Your brother will never come between us, ever. You are the sister I never had."

"Ohh, Bai," she cries, I wrap my arms around her and offer her the comfort she needs right now. Nancy walks over, I pull her into our hug, and the three of us stand there hugging and crying.

"Come on, ladies, let's get you home," Nate says.

The three of us pull apart. I take Nate's outstretched hand, while Wendy and Nancy link hands, and I find myself smiling at this. Together, we walk to Nate's car and he drives us home.

When Nate drops us off, I ask him to stay and he quickly agrees. After a quick shower, I change into my nightie and climb into my bed. While I wait for Nate to shower, I think about the last few days: the concert, Nate, William, and everything in between. This weekend has been perfect, absolutely perfect, even with what William did. I've never been so happy or content in my life. Nate comes into my room in nothing but a pair of boxers. My eyes rake over his body, and I find myself once again smiling.

Nate and I lie on my bed together. He pulls the duvet over us and we both relax. "Are you okay, Bailey?"

"I'm not sure. But having you here makes me feel safe."

"I'm happy to be here, and I can say without a doubt, I don't want to be anywhere else right now." He pauses. "When I saw him on top of you, my heart stopped and shattered at the same time. A force beyond my control overtook my body, and all I could think about was saving you. I'm sorry that happened. I should have protected you better."

"Nate, stop. It's not your fault. I'm fine, you did save me, and I will forever be grateful that you came along when you did."

"I just keep thinking, what-if and all the horrible

scenarios that could have taken place. I don't think my heart could handle losing you."

"You won't, Nate. I'm not going anywhere. Now that I've found you, I'm not going anywhere and I'm not letting you go." I snuggle into his side, we sigh in unison, but we are both so exhausted that we don't have the energy to laugh about it. The events of the last two days have finally caught up with us.

"I love you, Bai," Nate whispers into my hair before he gently kisses my temple. "Now and forever."

"I love you too, Nate. Now and forever," I whisper into his chest. I place a kiss over his heart, drape my arm across his chest, and burrow into his side. The beating of his heart lulls me happily to sleep. I'm tightly wrapped in the arms of the man of my dreams...literally.

...With a jolt, I'm snapped back to reality with my boss, Billy, yelling at me. I'm still holding the beers that I was handing to Nate. "Shit, sorry."

"It happened, didn't it?"

I nod my head, shocked that A. Nate is in front of me, and B. I was just accosted with a memory of us meeting. "Woodstock," I murmur.

Nate smiles. "*Titanic*. I remember meeting in London and being on the *Titanic* tog—"

"Get back to work, Bailey. Flirt later," her boss interrupts.

When he comes into view, I realize who he is. "William Clayton," I say.

"Billy, but yes that's my real name. Get back to work,

Bailey, and you," he points at Nate, "leave my staff alone."

Nate winks at me, before turning to Billy, "Clayton," he says in a deep baritone voice. Both Billy and I look to him in shock, its like we have heard him say that a thousand times before. Looking back at me, he softly adds, "I'll catch up with you later, Bai."

He picks up his beers and walks over to his friend, whom I later find out is Jason, Archie's cousin. He reminds me so much of Archie from when I met him at Woodstock, they even dress the same. Must be in the family genes.

For the rest of the night, I'm accosted with memories of Nate and me throughout the years. Meeting during the Depression, and overcoming everything to live until we were old and gray, dying within weeks of each other. Being trapped with Nate during the Great Fire of London in 1666, I didn't see the ending of that one, but I can guess how we died then. Drinking beer together at the first Oktoberfest in 1810.

We have met in many different times and we've lived many different lives together, but one thing has always remained the same, our love for one another.

Our love is endless.

Our love is unbreakable.

NATE

THE REST OF THE FUNCTION SEEMS TO FLY BY, BUT AT the same time it goes extremely slowly. Every time my eyes land on Bailey, I feel my cheeks heat and I'm flooded with more memories. I can't believe she's here. That she's real. I was starting to think I was going crazy. The dreams, well memories, were so vivid and now I know why.

I'm watching her behind the bar, when all of a sudden my view is blocked. Looking up I see Billy standing before me. "William Clayton, once again it's nice to see you," I sarcastically say, lifting my beer to my lips, I take a sip and continue to stare at him.

"Why?" he asks.

"Why what?" I reply in confusion.

"Why do you always get her? For as long as I can remember, she chooses you every-single-fucking-time. Why?"

"Probably cause you're a douche. You think of no one but yourself. You don't care who you trample, who your hurt, and that's why you always miss out." I pause. "Billy, when we were kids, you and I were friends, best friends, and just like in every life, over time you change and become this ass that no one likes. Most people tolerate you because of who your family is. Me, I don't giving a flying fuck about who your family is, and I think that's what pisses you off the most. Not that Bailey chooses me every time, but the fact that I don't bow to your feet. Maybe, just maybe, if you adjust your attitude, you too will be happy one of these days."

"You are full of shit, Winters."

"And your reply there proves my point."

"If we were still docked, I'd kick you off this boat. Stay away from my staff, especially Bailey." He turns away and stalks back to the bar. He stops and says something to Bai, her eyes snap to me before she looks back at Billy and says something in reply. Whatever she says pisses him off because he yells, "That's bullshit and you know it!" The entire boat goes quiet; all eyes flick to Bailey and Billy. He storms off, leaving Bailey standing by herself. She looks upset, so I walk over to her. "You okay, Bai?"

She nods her heads and swallows, "Yeah, nah, I'm fine. I'll um, ahh, get you two more beers."

Reaching out for Bailey, I grab her elbow and I when I touch her, a spark jolts us both. She spins around and looks at me, "Nate, thank you."

"For what?"

"For being here. I was lost and lonely. Drifting through life and in," she looks at her watch, "just over an hour, I feel more alive than I ever have. I know without a doubt it's because of you. I want nothing more than to get off this damn boat and start my life with you...again."

My face breaks out into the biggest smile. "And I want nothing more than to do that with you. Now, get back to work and as soon as we dock, we will ride off into the moonlight together."

"Sounds like a plan." She leans forward, places her lips against my cheek, and when she pulls back, my cheek is tingling. I zone out and I'm snapped back to reality when Bailey hands me two more beers. Before I can say anything, she gets back to work. From behind her I see William, and as usual, he's glaring at me. Raising one of the beers, I salute him with it before turning around and heading back to Jason.

"Do I even want to know?" he asks.

Shaking my head I say, "Nope. Let's just enjoy this cruise and then get back on dry land. I have a date."

Jason shakes his head at me but I don't care. I have a date with the most amazing girl in the world when we get back, and I could not be happier...I just hope this boat doesn't sink before I get to spend some time with my girl.

After what feels like an eternity, the boat finally docks. I walk over to Bailey and tell her that I'll wait for her. Billy, once again, glares at me. Jason teases me as we exit the boat. He hails a taxi and heads home. Resting my arms on the gangway railing, I eagerly await Bailey.

As each minute ticks by, I start to get nervous. My mind flits with question after question. What if she doesn't like me? What if she isn't really my Bailey? All different 'what-if' scenarios run through my mind, when all of a sudden, the hairs on the back of my neck stand on end. I've felt this before and without an ounce of doubt, I know that she is 'my' Bailey. No one else on this planet could invoke this feeling, and when I look up, I see her standing in the doorway. With the light from the boat behind her illuminating her beauty, she smiles at me and it radiates deep within me, and any remaining fears float away.

I'm about to step toward her when I notice Billy is standing behind her. He grabs Bailey by the elbow, halting her. He leans toward her, his eyes are locked on me and he says, loud enough for me to hear, "Are you sure you want to go with him?" He emphasizes the word *him*.

Bailey's eyes are locked on me, she nods her head and whispers, "Yes, it will always be yes when it comes to Nate." She spins toward Billy. "Billy, I can't explain it, but Nate is my everything. I don't exist without him, he's my other half. He always has been and he always will be." She steps toward him, kisses his cheek, when she pulls back, she adds, "Billy, I really hope you find your other half one of these days." He shakes his head, turns around, and storms back aboard the boat.

Bailey stares at the empty doorway for a few moments. I notice her shoulders hunch in sadness, but then she turns around. Her eyes lock on mine and she smiles. She reaches for the gangway railing and starts walking to me. And as usual with Bailey, I'm compelled to come to her, and I put one foot in front of the other and walk toward her.

We stand facing one another, both of us breathing deeply. We stare at one another and she smiles at me. Reaching up, she cups my cheek and whispers, "It really is you."

Lifting my hand, I cup her cheek and my thumb gently strokes her silky soft skin. "And it's really you," I softly murmur back.

A force beyond my control overtakes me and I slide my hand behind her head and pull her to me. I grip her cheeks in my palms, and I slam my lips to hers, for our millionth first kiss. My tongue seeks access to her mouth and this kiss is just like I remember. It's full of passion, heat, and desire. It's Bailey and me from my dreams, from our past.

We pull apart and she whispers, "Wow, so much better in real life."

We both laugh. And her laugh is just as I remember.

Lacing our fingers together, we walk along the jetty back up to dry land. "Bai, do you, ummm, errr, wa—"

"Yes, a thousand times yes," she says.

"You don't even know what I was going to say."

She shrugs her shoulders. "It doesn't matter, I just want to be with you. Nate, I can't explain it, but I just know that you and I are meant to be together. And I know that I don't know you, but I do know you. If that makes sense."

Nodding my head in agreement, I smile because I agree with her one hundred and fifty percent. "It makes perfect sense to me, Bailey. Come on, let's go."

Bailey and I hail a taxi and we head back to her place, since she lives by herself. This night started out with me alone, but it ends with the woman of my dreams, literally and figuratively, and I could not be happier.

EPILOGUE

Bailey and Nate are fated to meet in every life.

Their souls deeply entwined.

No hurdle to great to climb. No ocean too deep. No concert too wild.

Their destiny is written in the stars—the past, the present, and in the future.

No matter where they are or what they are doing, they will always find each other; their antecedent love.

THE END!!!!

Read on for a sneak peek at Out of Nowhere, a second chance contemporary small town romance.

PROLOGUE

BANG!

The sound of the gunfire is deafening, it echoes through my head, my ears ringing. People are running for their lives, screaming in terror, but I stand here frozen, my body unable to move as a mixture of fear, disbelief, and shock courses through my veins.

Standing in the middle of the path, I watch the scene unfold in front of me. I'm unable to do anything to stop what's happening before me.

BANG!

All of a sudden, I'm tumbling to the ground and I land with a thud on my stomach. Brian's body is half on top of mine. With a shove, I push him off me and roll over onto my back. Lying there dazed, I stare up at the sky. Everything around me is muffled, my vision blurred. I let out the breath that I didn't realize I was holding, and wince in pain. People screaming and the sound of feet pounding the pavement as people run for their lives snaps me back to reality, and it's a reality that I don't want to be in.

With a groan, I look to my side and see my fiancé lying there, his lifeless eyes staring back at me. The loving gaze from before replaced with a vacant dead stare, and behind him I see carnage everywhere I look.

In an instant, my life imploded.

One minute I was happy and living the picture-perfect life: great job, wonderful fiancé, loving family, amazing friends. Life in the city could not have been better, and in the blink of an eye, nothing would be the same again. My job, gone. My fiancé and family ripped from my life. I am alone, lost, and unhappy. The city I once loved—now a painful reminder of everything I no longer have. One day, I make a decision that would change the path of my future.

On a whim, I pack a bag, switch off my phone, and take off. I leave my shattered life behind and embark on an adventure to find myself. My journey comes to a halt when a force beyond my control pulls me in a different direction and I land in the quaint country town of Nels Cove, Colorado. There is something about this small town that speaks to me. It is nothing like New York, but here I am happy and start to feel like me again. After only a few days I decide to stay and it's in Nels Cove that I get my life back.

Out of Nowhere is available to buy or read with you kindle unlimited subscriptions.

ACKNOWLEDGMENTS

Firstly I need to thank **Leigh Stone** for inviting me to participate in the Titanic anthology. I wasn't sure I could write a story about the Titanic but once I sat down BAM, Bailey and Nate came to life. And then I extended their story and I fell in love with them and Woodstock.

Thank you to my hubby, **Troy**. You are my rock and my saving grace. Thank you for loving me and encouraging me daily. Our lil' munchkins, **Piper** and **Kade**. You both are my greatest achievements and I'm lucky to have you both as my kids.

Cheers and thank you to **Amy, Amanda, Beth, Crissy, Halle, Megan and Shez – my beta babes**. You ladies take the time to read what I send and give me your honest opinions. I value the support and encouragement that you give me. Thank you, thank you for everything. Love you ladies, like I love wine; hard!

To my editor and friend, **Karen Hrdlicka**

(**Barren Acres Editing**) – you have been with me since the beginning and with your help I have grown as an author, without your support I wouldn't be where I am today. You are amazing at what you do and thank you for suggesting I extend the original story. I look forward to the day that we finally meet.

Thank you to R.L. Kenderson for the new cover. As soon as I saw it, I knew it was the one for Antecedent's makeover. I'm sorry for all the tweaks and requests but I'm so happy with the final product. I also need to thank, **Müjde Özcaner** from **Way to Love Design,** for the original cover.

Thank you to **Virginia Tesi Carey,** you checked over my baby and you ensured that I dotted my I's and crossed my T's.

And finally, **my readers**. Thank you, once again for reading and supporting me throughout my authoring journey.

ANTECEDENT PLAYLIST

Dark and Stormy – Ash
Leave Out All The Rest – Linkin Park
Stay With Me – Sam Smith
Chasing Cars – Snow Patrol
Mirrors – Justin Timberlake
For The First Time – The Script
Underneath Your Clothes – Shakira
Nothing Really Matters – Mr. Probz
Say Something – A Great Big World
A Thousand Years – Christina Perri
Skinny Love – Birdy
Little Things – One Direction
How Long Will I Love You – Ellie Goulding
Love You Like A Love Song – Selena Gomez & The
Scene
Waterfall – Stargate, Pink, Sia
Sober – Pink
Letters From The Sky – Civil Twilight

The Trick Is To Keep Breathing – Garbage
Unchained Melody – The Righteous Brothers
The Unforgiven III – Metallica
Purple Haze – Jimi Hendrix
Foxey Lady – Jimi Hendrix
Proud Mary – Creedence Clearwater Revival
Lover Her Madly – The Doors
Evil Ways - Santana

This playlist can be found on Spotify.

Oasis

Unequivocal Love

Five Words

Broken Rules

...and a few more as well.

THE UNEXPECTED SERIES

When it comes to love, expect the unexpected

The Unexpected Gift

The Unexpected Letter

The Unexpected Package

The Unexpected Connection

THE LIQUOR CABINET SERIES

Liquor has never been so disturbingly saucy

Malt Me (Book 1)

Tequila Healing (Book 2)

Wine Not (Book 3)

The Final Shot (Book 4)

The Liquor Cabinet: Series boxset

ABOUT THE AUTHOR

DL Gallie is from Queensland, Australia, but she's lived in many different places all over the world, including the UK and Canada. She currently resides in Central Queensland with her husband and two munchkins. She and her husband have been together since she was sixteen, and although they drive each other crazy at times, she couldn't imagine her life without him.

Shortly after her son was born, DL began reading again. With encouragement from her husband, she picked up the pen and started writing, and now the voices in her head won't shut up.

DL enjoys listening to music, drinking white wine in the summer, red wine in the winter, and beer all year round. She's also never been known to turn down a cocktail, especially a margarita.